PADMAMALI

PADMAMALI

Umesh Chandra Sarkar

Translated by
Snehaprava Das

BLACK EAGLE BOOKS
Dublin, USA | Bhubaneswar, India

 Black Eagle Books
USA address:
7464 Wisdom Lane
Dublin, OH 43016

India address:
E/312, Trident Galaxy, Kalinga Nagar,
Bhubaneswar-751003, Odisha, India

E-mail: info@blackeaglebooks.org
Website: www.blackeaglebooks.org

First International Edition Published by
Black Eagle Books, 2024

PADMAMALI
by **Umesh Chandra Sarkar**
Translated by **Snehaprava Das**

Translation Copyright © Snehaprava Das

Cover & Interior Design: Ezy's Publication

ISBN- 978-1-64560-615-4 (Paperback)

Printed in the United States of America

Foreword

Padmamali, the first novel in Oriya, was published in 1888. Early reviews of the novel, the author's self-defense combine to invest the appearance of the first full-length work of prose fiction in Oriya with immense cultural significance. The first readers and critics of the novel recognized that something, something radically different had been attempted in *Padmamali*.

The author, Umesh Chandra Sarkar (1857-1914) was also conscious and confident of the fact that he was something of a pioneer, that he had done something for which no precedent existed in the history of Oriya literature. Conscious of the limitations of available critical vocabulary in Oriya, he described his work in English as 'a historical romance of the feudatory states'. The role of the author as historian, an objective truth-teller was restated more aggressively in the preface to the second edition of the novel. In this the author seeks to define and defend an emergent genre, not fully independent of traditional narrative conventions, but at the same time absorbing and getting shaped by the conventions of the western realistic novel.

Sarkar's remarks in the preface to the second edition of *Padmamali* seem to have been provoked by a couple of adverse early reviews. Contemporary attacks on *Padmamali* focused on two 'flaws' in the novel: a) errors of language and infelicities of expression resulting from the author's unsure grasp of Oriya and from the influence of Bengali on his prose style; b) errors of taste. In the opinion of the reviewers, the author displayed bad taste in his description of love at first sight between the central characters, and in the portrayal of the abbot of the monastery. To the first charge Sarkar responded by saying a language cannot remain fixed forever and that he had enriched Oriya language by making it express new modes of feeling. To the second and more serious charge that he had violated norms of good taste, Sarkar's response was more assertive and interesting: he stated that he was an historian, not a moralist or the writer of farces, who aimed at reforming the morals of a society. He had simply recorded what he had seen and his portrayal of the abbot's character was therefore fully justified. This lively debate over the form and content of *Padmamali* indicates that a discerning readership was already in existence in Orissa towards the end of the nineteenth century, a readership exposed to new art forms and new artistic conventions and yet not completely averse to or alienated from traditional narrative conventions.

Before *Padmamali* appeared on the literary scene in Orissa, a few attempts had been made at writing fictional narratives in prose in Oriya. However, none of these had led to the composition of full-length novels and they exist only as fragments. It is significant that two of these unfinished narratives were set in a specific past time: *Saudamini* (1878) was set in the period of Mughal rule and *Anathini* in the reign of Prataparudra Dev, in the sixteenth century. Interestingly, Sarkar resisted the pull of the remote past, refused to embark on what Meenakshi Mukherjee calls a voyage of nostalgia and chose to set *Padmamali* in the recent past, in a feudatory state in British India.

At one level, *Padmamali* is unmistakably a romantic tale involving the adventures of beautiful and virtuous young lovers belonging to the upper strata of Oriya society. The action of the narrative at this level revolves round the meeting, separation and reunion of the lovers. The plot consists of two abductions, a secret betrothal, two rescue attempts, a trial, and a marriage. The beautiful daughter of a court official in the kingdom of Nilagiri is abducted by the king's brother-in-law. She is rescued by the king of Kaptipada, a neighbouring kingdom, and they fall in love at first sight. They get betrothed secretly in a monastery after the king overcomes initial reservations about marrying beneath his station. The villain makes another attempt at making the heroine his own by getting her father arrested and carrying her off for the second time. This time the king of Kaptipada attacks Nilagiri with the help of an aspirant to the throne and rescues his beloved. The villain is punished and the British authorities take a lenient view of the act of transgression on the part of the king of Kaptipada and the lovers live happily ever after. It is obvious that stock narrative conventions shape the narrative at this level. There are distinct echoes in the narrative of the epics, the Mahabharat and the Ramayan: the name of the villain is Duryodhan and the garden where the heroine is kept confined after being abducted for the second time is called Ashok. All obstacles blocking the lovers' union are eventually removed as they find allies from unexpected quarters. Inconvenient characters are speedily dispatched by co-operating circumstances and providence brings the lovers succour whenever they need it desperately.

Read purely at this level, the novel lends little support to Sarkar's claim that he was a pioneer. What makes it difficult for one to reduce *Padmamali* to a conventional romance with a thin overlay of historical incidents is a number of complicating factors that call for close scrutiny. It was of course not possible for Sarkar to break completely with pre-novel conventions. In her groundbreaking study of novel and society in India, Meenakshi Mukherjee has convincingly demonstrated why effecting such a break was difficult in India. At the same time, writing conventional romance became increasingly difficult and early novelists in India tried to accommodate, conflicting claims of romance and realism within the same work of fiction.

The presence of a moralizing, intrusive and garrulous narrator in *Padmamali* allows its author to negotiate the conflicting demands of romance and realism. The narrator of the first novel in Oriya is acutely conscious of the presence of a readership that is unwilling to suspend disbelief. This accounts for the awkward explanations offered by a self-conscious narrator for unconvincing behaviour on the part of characters who actually belong to the world of romance. The intellectual and imaginative world inhabited by the narrator is visibly larger than the one in which the characters of the novel live and move. The narrator is conscious of the limits imposed by colonial rule on the choices of characters who express themselves in a rhetoric more appropriate in a romance. It is through the interventions of the narrator that the once-upon-a-time in the novel gives way to the here-and-now. An attempt, albeit clumsy, is often made by the narrator in course of the narrative to locate characters in a concrete and believable historical milieu. The action of the novel begins in a sacred space but finds resolution in the court of a colonial magistrate. It is the narrator who deftly guides the reader away from the timeless world of romance towards the world of history.

Thus, what distinguishes the first novel in Oriya is

the manipulation of the conventions of romance to open up a space for realism. True, the characters do not achieve individuality and remain bound by predictable moral and social codes but their uneasy relationship with these codes has been made evident by an intrusive narrator. Characters belonging to a non-aristocratic background display a remarkable degree of freedom and vitality which anticipate the vibrant social realism of Fakir Mohan Senapati's novels. In short, the foundation of realistic prose fiction was laid by Sarkar, who dramatized the difficulties of writing conventional romance in a world reshaped by the realities of colonial rule.

Jatindra Kumar Nayak

Introduction

An Imaginative Work

Published in 1888, *Padmamali*, by Umesh Chandra Sarkar, is said to be the first novel in Oriya. The sense in which *Padmamali* can be claimed to be a novel is complicated, however, by the fact that it intertwines strands from traditional genres with the novel form, mixing the old with the new, marking both continuity and innovation. It is perhaps precisely this generic hybridity which has led to *Padmamali* being considered the first novel, since while it is both a romance and a chronicle it is also more than either of these.

If *Padmamali* were only the story of the love of two prominent, eminently virtuous and self-sacrificing people for each other and their ability, finally, to successfully overcome the obstacles placed in the way of their love, then it would probably be of only minor interest to the modern reader. There is little development of psychological detail, and the events affecting the two lovers - *Padmamali* and the king of Kaptipada, Parikshita Singh -take place, at least on the interpersonal level, in a world of absolute good and evil.

In addition to this love story, however, there is the backdrop of real historical events, which introduce into the story the complexity of reality and undermine the absolute dichotomies. This historical dimension is the second strand in *Padmamali*, and the author, in his prefaces and in the novel itself, proclaims its importance and the conformity of his narrative to it. Thus more than merely a romance *Padmamali* is also a chronicle. As a result, good and evil no longer constitute the operative categories; political and social concerns complicate, contaminate, pluralize and undermine them. The references to the presence of the British in India, and in particular to the British magistrate, Ricketts, are an important part of this density of historical fact Thus· Mahanta Harihara Ramanuja Das, whose power is that of a ruler and whose role in the novel is essentially to caution behaviour which otherwise might seem scandalous or unorthodox, professes a certain confidence in the magistrate, saying: "I have heard that a magistrate named Sir Ricketts is now in charge of Balasore. He is a good administrator and quite concerned with the well-being of his subjects." Despite this confidence placed in him, Ricketts nevertheless remains very much on the outside of society and events and is shown attempting to impose his will in a situation that he does hot completely understand, let alone master, even if, as stated in the Epilogue, he takes "a lot of pains to arrive at the truth". Thus when he is informed by the Mahanta of the reasons why Parikshita Singh had joined the rebel forces against the Queen of Nilagiri Ricketts somewhat petulantly reverses his decision to place the king in jail, asking why he had not been made aware of the situation. There is a certain amount of ambivalence in the representation of the colonial presence, seen as introducing both a measure of justice and a degree of foreignness. This latter is underlined at various points in the novel, for example when the narrator, similar in this to the narrator of *Chha Mana Atha Guntha*, equates knowledge of English - that is, the presence of the English - with undesirable social change:

During the period in which this narrative has been set, the young folk, unlike their modern counterparts, had no knowledge of English and therefore they had not learnt to forsake moral conduct and decorum of behaviour. They did not arrogantly denounce their forefathers as stupid. At that time modern principles and theories were not in vogue, and people were orthodox in their outlook on life. (Chapter 7)

The theme of the increasing decadence of nineteenth-century society often recurs in Fakir Mohan Senapati's writing as well, and here it is explicitly linked to the British presence, metonymically signalled by the reference to the English language. Another instance in which this presence is marked as foreign and invasive is in Chapter 13, where native doctors are called in to succour love-sick *Padmamali*. In a total absence of idealization of the 'native' the chapter pungently satirizes these doctors and their self-importance, but it also marks as unacceptable an alternative solution, which would have been to ask the civil surgeon, a British functionary, to examine her. Here is how the narrator characterizes such a possibility: "Some friends of the landlord, who had developed a modern outlook, advised him to call in the civil surgeon from Balasore. But how would that have been possible? How could a beef- and pork-eating Englishman enter a holy Hindu house wearing leather shoes to take a look at an unmarried girl and prescribe for her a diet of wine and meat! That could never be permitted. Most of his friends, orthodox in temperament, disapproved of the proposal, and it was dropped." 'Modern' and 'English' are opposed to 'orthodox' and 'Hindu', with value accorded not the first but the second. Nevertheless, their very opposition points to the social change underway in Orissa at the time. Most notably the sentence beginning "How could...." accumulates a number of transgressions against social and religious taboos involved in the meeting of English and Hindu, and marks both the chasm separating the two and the inherent violence underlying the colonial presence.

The third strand in *Padmamali* makes the text something other than either a romance or a chronicle - that is, a novel - and is composed of the references by the narrator to telling a story. The author's prefaces of 1888 and 1912 insist on both the novel's relation to actual historical events and on the imaginative nature of the work. The Preface to the First Edition (1888) speaks of "writing a work of prose fiction that is the product of one's imagination", but a fiction "based on historical facts". Twenty-four years later, in the Preface to the "significantly improved and enlarged" second edition-changes which justify an increase in price-the author characterizes *Padmamali* as an "historical novel" while insisting on the novel's accuracy: "While relating these events, I have taken enough care to provide readers with entertainment without attempting even the slightest distortion of historical truth." A record of events, *Padmamali* is also written to entertain, and the three strands of romance, chronicle and narration interwoven, each playing against but also reinforcing the others, as in the first paragraph of Chapter 23:

Being faithful to history is difficult, but when relating historical events a writer has no options but to perform that task in all honesty. I have only done that. The events narrated in the previous chapters demonstrate that to accomplish the evil intention of one wicked man several innocent persons were subjected to torture and suffering. Sensitive readers, while going through the previous chapters, must have felt terribly upset: the chords of their hearts must have throbbed with the strains of sympathy and sorrow. I request them to forgive me. I have already said that a writer has no authority to distort historical truth; even the most marginal alterations are not permitted. If by relating the sorrowful incidents in the previous chapters I have been instrumental in bringing readers unhappiness and causing them to become angry, I offer my humble apologies and seek their permission to proceed with my story.

Demonstrating an awareness of the process of telling a story and of its effect on potential readers, the narrator conflates the elements of romance ("the evil intention of the wicked man") and of chronicle, presenting the story as having been dictated by historical events. Absolving the author of all responsibility, the narrator presents his story as pure historical truth, to which even the most marginal alterations are not permitted. In affirming this, however the narrator also insists on the nature of the text as 'relation', 'narration' and 'story'-an insistence that contradicts the absolute faithfulness to history and echoes the Preface of 1888, which presents *Padmamali* as a product both of the writer's imagination and of historical fact. As such it justifies the claim made for it as the first novel in Oriya.

Paul St-Pierre

Preface to the First Edition

During the tough time Literature of Utkal is passing through at present, writing a fictional text would undoubtedly be a bold venture. I have made up my mind to take up the challenge. Despite being aware that my lack of proficiency in the vernacular and a limited command over the Odia vocabulary might subject me to ridicule, I have set out to embark on this venture. I may or may not be successful in the mission, but having made up my mind once, it will not be possible for me to step back. The mission has a dual purpose; it aims at enhancing the glory of the Literature of Utkal and at the same time entertaining the readers. Even if the mission fails, the very thought that I had pursued such a noble goal will bring me peace in the hours of despair and distress.

As far as my knowledge goes, not a single novel founded on historical facts has been written in Odia till now. For a sensitive writer, interested in the study of the history of Utkal, there is no dearth of facts or resources for writing a historical fiction. I have based my text on some incidents occurring in a not-so-prominent colonial state of Odisha in a given span of time. In case my effort proves vain and inconsequential, young men of better literary caliber than mine, following the path I have shown would attain success and adequately recompense my failure to enrich and glorify the literature of Utkal.

Dhenkanal   **Sri Umesh Chandra Sarkar**
19th October, 1888

Preface To The Second Edition

Padmamali is the only historical novel written in the Odia vernacular till date. Though published first about half a century ago, not another narrative of the kind to match Padmamali, to my knowledge, has yet been added to the volume of Odia literature during this long span. The central story of Padmamali juxtaposes two contemporary historical events. One of them is the attack launched on the province of Panchagada by the officials of the princely state of Nilagiri and the other is the invasion of the fort of Nilagiri by Harihara Bhramarabara babu. Scholars interested in the history of ancient Odisha could discover the significance of both the incidents with a little effort. Subsequently a number of other episodes like the historical background of the state of Nilagiri, the village of Panchagada getting free from the rulership of Nilagiri and coming under the British governance, the trial of the criminals who had marauded Panchagada and of the rebels who attacked Nilagiri, by the Magistrate of Balasore Sir Henry Ricketts and some such details are incorporated into the main story. On one hand, I have put in my best efforts to entertain the readers and had desisted from distorting the historical truth even marginally, on the other. The present edition is a further corrected and a bit enlarged version of the previous edition. It is left to the readers to decide if those changes have succeeded or not in enhancing the beauty of the text. Since the size of the text is slightly enlarged, we are compelled to make a proportionate increase in its price.

Fort of Talcher   Sri Umesh Chandra Sarkar
17. 11. 1912

Preface to the Third Edition

To say that Padmamali is the only historical novel written in Odia will not be an overstatement. Because of its immense popularity amongst the readers a second edition of the novel was printed in the Kishor Printing Press at Talcher Gada. The second editions of the book too were sold away in a short time. It was decided to bring out a third edition at the special request of some generous friends and enthusiastic readers. Hence a carefully and meticulously edited and a slightly larger version of the novel was printed in my newly founded Lakshmi Narayana Printing Press incurring heavy expenses and with hard labour to fulfill the need of the readers. My efforts will be amply rewarded if everyone buys a copy of this book.

I am an ordinary writer and a publisher. It is a well-known fact that some books written by me are printed in other printing presses. The second edition of the two of those books, Maharaja Panchama George (King George V) and Khana Bachana (The Sayings of the Stutterer) have been brought out. The second edition of the other books are also expected to come out soon.

Kazi Bazar   Sri Bimalacharana Ray Choudhury
6.6. 30   Proprietor
Cuttack

Preface to the Fourth Edition

The repute of Odia fiction had attained a great height today. But that should not make us forget the inception of the same. While discussing the growth and progress of Odia fiction the major role of the narrative Padmamali in the context must be taken into account. It has made its first appearance in Dhenkanal in the year 1888. It appeared again in Talcher in the year 1912. The third edition of the novel was brought out in the year1930 in Cuttasck. And once again the fourth edition is going to appear this year, 1962. The repeated publishing of the book bears testimony to its great popularity.

The plot of the novel is apparently founded on two historical events like the attack on Panchagada by the officials of the princely state of Nilagiri and the invasion of Nilagiri by Harihara Bhramarabara and his associates. But the author has displayed an exceptional narratorial innovativeness blending history into romance through a delineation of the romantic issues centering around the life of Padmamali. The historical reality of Panchagada getting free from the governance of the king of Nilagiri and coming under the category of special estates under the direct control of the British is skillfully woven into an ambience of romance in order to enhance the aesthetic appeal of the novel.

As the first ever novel written in Odia vernacular Padmamali demands a unique and special recognition not just in the domain of Odia novel, but that of Odia literature as a whole. It was included in the syllabus of the Calcutta University and still continues to be there in the curriculum of the Post Graduation course in Odia in the Utkal University. Padmamali has created its own identity and is in no need of an introduction.

Umesh Chandra:

Umesh Chandra was born in Puri in the year 1857. His father Ishwar Chandra Sarkar was a loyal inspector of police under the government. Umesh Chandra was the youngest among the three children, two sons and a daughter. Unfortunately Umesh Chandra lost his father when he was only two. After his father's death Unesh Chandra moved to Cuttack along with his mother and siblings. They settled in the house at Kazi Bazar in Cuttack and Umesh Chandra, with the support of his kinsfolk, completed graduation and thereafter joined the office of the Commissioner of Odisha. By dint of his sincerity and sharp wit he was promoted to the post of the Assistant Manager of Dhenkanal and then to the post o Manager of Kanika and Talcher. At that time those estates or zamindaris were under the Court of Wards. Padmamali was published in 1888 during his stay at Dhenkanal. He suffered from serious ailments while working in Kanika and was compelled to take voluntary retirement from the office in the year 1899. He stayed at his house in Kazi Bazar at Cuttack. After recovering from illness, he devoted himself to the service of Odia literature. His play 'Jattoh Dharma Tattoh Jaya (Victory is there where Justice Is) during this period. He had published two texts Odia Bhasa ra Dhaga Dhamali (Odia proverbs) and Mahimna Stava (Prayers to the Almighty) under a pseudonym during the same period. He had, under the pseudonym of Udasha, was publishing serialized versions of a play Kendujhar Vidroha (Mutiny in Kendujhar) in a periodical titled Mukura. The play however, could not be completed.

Umesh Chandra had enough proficiency in English language too. Worth mentioning among the English texts he had written are, Easy Way to Learn English, Part 1; Temple of Truth, and Speaking the Truth. He has also made a rhymed translation of Hitopadesha (Noble Advices) into English, but the book could not be published for lack of funds.

In the last part of his life poverty compelled him to join the job of an auditor in the court of the king of Talcher, in the year i911. While still in service there, Umesh Chandra succumbed to diarrhoea in the year 1914.

We present the first creation of this noble devotee of literature to the readers once again with a hope that they will understand and acknowledge its special significance.

Cuttack   Sincerely
19. 8 .62   The Publisher

Chapter I

The Festival of Jagara

On the fourteenth day of the dark fortnight of the month of *Falguna,* in the year 1834, the small town of Manatira (known all over as Mantri), situated in the southern part of Mayurbhanja district, was crowded with people arriving from many places. People, young and old, including kids and women, poured into the town. No other sound, except the hubbub of the crowd, was audible. Who could keep count of those who came and went? The girls, adorning their shapely figures with sarees that had been stored carefully in the caskets, arrived here to earn merit for this life and the life after, through the worship of Vaidyanath, the lord of the gods. A group of women, intending to reach the interiors of the temple, had passed through the main entrance and were waiting for their turn to step into the jagamohan or the assembly hall of the temple. Groups of men and women, desperate in their eagerness to get through the narrow door to reach the jagamohan of the temple, were squeezed from all sides, while the canes of the temple attendants fell on their defenceless backs. It is said, the crowd here used to be so thick on the auspicious occasion of Sivaratri that once a pregnant woman had had a miscarriage in the stampede.

Crossing the jagamohan with a lot of difficulty, the pilgrims reached the bhoga mandapa, the hall for residuary offerings. The place inspired fear. Darkness sheltered here as if hiding from the sun, the way an owl hides itself from sunlight at midday. It was closed on all other sides and there was no proper ventilation. A pungent odour emitting from the compressed air stung the nostrils. However, one can never attain happiness without enduring pain. Virtue is the reward of suffering. People from far-off places, after completing an arduous journey, had arrived here only to have a glimpse of Lord Vaidyanath. But they had to face one trouble after another. The traveler forgot the pains of the journey when he had a glimpse of the trident on the spire of the temple from a distance; but his agony did not end there. Having survived the suffocating rush in the jagamohan and the blows of the cane, when, at last he reached the bhoga mandapa, he heaved a sigh of relief thinking that Lord Vaidyanath had put an end to his sufferings; but soon his spirit sank. Nothing was visible in the dark; the crowd was as thick as before. After descending the slippery steps that led from the narrow doors of the bhoga mandapa, with great pain, he would get a blurred view of the idol of Lord Shiva. His eyes could discern, in the poor light of the lamps, a worn out, blackened canopy hanging over the idol of Goddess Parvati. The devotees, praying for the wellbeing of their near and dear ones, offered water and milk to be poured on the idol of Lord Shiva.

A group of women, from the village of Panchagada, which was under the rule of Nilagiri Quilla, had also come to have a darshan of the Lord. They came out of the temple after they had set their eyes on the Lord. There was a woman of thirty-two in the group, whose costume and bashful elegance bore testimony to the fact that she belonged to a respectable family. She was very shy by nature and had a long veil drawn over her head. Despite her best efforts to keep the veil on her head, it occasionally slid down and revealed the loveliness of her face. The woman was in the fullness of her youth. The radiance of her beauty, like a lotus in full bloom, shoved through her silk saree. Clothes are used to cover the body. But her silk saree, on which pictures of swans were printed, could not conceal the beautiful curves in her body. But now we are not concerned with this lady. It would be enough to mention that this lady had married the landlord of Panchagada, Jagabandhu Pattnaik and made him a fortunate man.

Behold the girl beside her. Young *Padmamali* stood by her mother. Her eyes darted here and there in childish inquisitiveness. The young girl and the lady, locked like two lotuses -- one in full bloom and the other beginning to open up. The human heart is eternally thirsty for beauty. When an object of extraordinary beauty meets our eye, it inspires amazement; the amazement turns into a joy of appreciation. But having observed it for a long time, our senses experience satiety and our eyes lose interest in that object. But the sight that presented itself was not the one of that kind. It excited wonder at the first glance, which led to joy and thereafter, a new feeling arose. The look in a human eye can be innocent and undefiled; it can also be prurient and lustful. Seen with virtuous eyes, everything created by the supreme architect seems pure and holy, but evil ones see the entire world as infernal and devilish. Both the virtuous and vicious ones viewed this beautiful sight before us. Both were filled with joy. But the joy that filled the virtuous one's heart was pure; it was a joy that made him praise the creative power of the Maker. He wondered,

'If His creation could be so beautiful, how beautiful the Creator must be!' The evil one also beheld the beauty but his heart was overcome with wanton lust.

As I feel myself incapable of depicting the beauty of Padmamali, I quote here from the great poet Kalidasa:

"Having passed the phase of childhood
On the threshold of the next she stood;
Youth -- is a natural adornment
On her slender figure s
Which, though not wine, could intoxicate.
Like an arrow from "Kama's" bow it could work,
Even without its flowers
The same passion it could evoke."

After quoting this stanza I believe that it would be enough if the reader considers Padmamali as beautiful as his own wife, who has stepped into the next phase of childhood, i.e. youth. If we dwell on her beauty for long, the reader, feeling that I hold Padmamali to be more beautiful than his wife, may take offence. O' wise reader, your wife may be a thousand times more beautiful than Padmamali but you must keep it in mind that I now write Padmamali's story. When I bring myself to write the story of your wife I promise to do my best to portray her to the public truthfully.

Padmamali was sixteen. Her youthful beauty was like a lotus bud, whose petals were about to open up. Her face shone with a graceful radiance. Wise men differ in their response to a beautiful face. But in my opinion, the beauty of a face depends much on the eyes of the beholder. Under the slightly curved brows, lovely like ones painted with an artist's brush, her large, lotus like eyes could stir the onlooker's heart, with their slanting glances. They-beamed with a soft radiance. Her smooth lovely forehead, large eyes, sharp nose, berry-red lips, the creases that appeared on her forehead when she laughed and her fine features could have inspired a Greek sculptor. As she was the only issue of her wealthy parents, she was reared with great love and care. Perhaps, for this reason her face retained a childlike fickleness. This fickleness, adding to her beauty, made her face look more captivating. The shapeliness of her slender figure, dressed in a silk saree, was like the arrow of Kama, the god of love, without its flowers.

Padmamali's mother and the ladies in their group came out of the temple and sat down at a place outside. Each of them lighted a day-lamp to observe the nightly vigil of the Jagara festival (the devotees have to keep awake through the night and keep the lamp burning). A young man, around thirty years of age, came out after them and standing at a distance watched the group.

During such grand festivals, where a number of girls assemble, many young men, intoxicated with the fervour of youth, come there to feast their eyes on their beauty. This young man was one among them. His eyes kept roving till they fell on Padmamali. He followed her thereafter.

He came out of the temple, stood still like a puppet for a while; then apprehending that his surreptitious movements might evoke suspicion, he walked down to a mango tree nearby and sat down under it. He sat there for some time looking a bit absent-minded. After a while when his companion came to him and told him that he would show him a beautiful girl, he said:

"What better sight could you show me than the one I have already seen?"

He pointed to the place where Padmamali stood.

His companion went in that direction and returned soon afterwards. "Yes; you are right. Such a beaty is rarely seen in the three worlds," he commented.

"Balabantaray, this girl has to be snatched tonight."

"Tonight! How can that be possible? There is such a big crowd. Moreover, Routray is present here with two hundred soldiers. You can tell from her looks, the girl does not hail from an ordinary family." The later sounded hesitant.

"Are you afraid? Don't you know that once I am drawn towards something, I must have it by all means?" asked the young man.

'"Well, let us see; it depends on the wish of Lord Vaidyanath."

As Balabantaray spoke, a shadow fell across both of them and quickly melted away. Padmamali, her heart filled with premonitions, nervously watched these young men.

It was past midnight. The pilgrims waited for the moment when the Mahadeepa would be raised. (On the occasion of Sivaratri a large lamp of ghee is raised to the spire of the temple of Lord Siva). They would return home after the ceremony was over. A few would spend the night in the temple premises.

It was the night of the fourteenth day of the dark fortnight. The sky was overcast with clouds. Not a single star was visible. Suddenly a voice announced: "Mahadeepa is going to be raised." All eyes turned in the direction of the temple. A Brahmin, holding a large burning ghee lamp in his right hand, his left hand clutching the iron chain hanging from the crest of the temple for support, climbed the steps that went up to the spire of the temple. He had reached almost the top of the temple when the sound of a loud rumbling was heard and the rain began pouring in torrents.

Pandemonium broke out. The spectators ran here and there in search of shelter. Taking advantage of the commotion, the two young men, whom I have mentioned before, grabbed Padmamali and hurried down the Kansari Street.

Chapter II

Padmamali's Release

The young man and his follower carried Padmamali and strode along the Kansari Street. Banchhanidhi Balabantaray lifted the girl's unconscious body, still as a corpse, over his strong muscular shoulder and moved effortlessly. They walked for about half an hour in this manner.

The rain eased off, but the darkness was thick as before. Frequent flashes of lightning helped the travellers to find their ways to their destination. After half an hour's walk, discovering faint signs of life returning to the girl's inert body, Balabantaray felt relieved. He realised that they were totally safe there and suggested that they must rest for a while. His companion eagerly accepted the suggestion and sat down on a rock. He lifted Padmamali to his lap. Slowly, consciousness seeped back to the girl's body.

It is left to the reader to imagine the distress of the girl when she discovered herself in the custody of strangers, in the pitch darkness of the night, helpless and alone in an alien place.

Fear and shame overcame her when she found herself in the lap of a stranger. She extricated herself from his arms and sat down on the ground. Her meagre strength would not have enabled her to free herself from the strong arms of the young man, but her abductor, aware of her desire to be free, did not stop her.

She remained silent for some time. The young man and his companion did not say anything either. Padmamali surveyed her present condition. Then she mustered up courage and asked boldly:

"Who are you? Why have you brought me here?"

"Beautiful one," said the young man. "When I set my eyes on you for the first time in the temple of Lord Vaidyanath, I laid down my youth and my wealth at your feet. I would kill myself unless you cast a loving glance at me. I would have lost my will to live if I had not got you. I, therefore, took you away from your kins. You must forgive me. Look upon me as your slave. I am your vassal. You need not have any cause of fear from me. I am the chief of the kingdom of Nilagiri. Siva Pattnaik is the dewan of Nilagiri only in name. From this day I offer my wealth and my youth at your lovely feet. Have mercy on me just for once. Reward me with a look of love."

Having made this long statement, the young man caught hold of Padmamali's feet and tried to win her over making humble prayers.

Padmamali: "I am a subject in the state of which you are the chief. It does not behove you to trouble me in this way. I am a humble subject. It is improper to hold my feet. Please leave them."

The young man released her feet and said:

"I am glad to know that you are a subject of Nilagiri. Never think for a moment that I am a tyrant and that I intend to do you any harm. My good senses deserted me when I set my eyes on you. Please forgive me if I had been rude to you in any way because I was not in my senses. If you accept me, you will command the same respect and honour that the queen of Nilagiri does. With such thoughts in my mind I have taken you away from your relatives. Please forgive me if you think it is a crime."

Padmamali: You seem to be wise and judicious. You are the chief of the state of Nilagiri. Does bringing me here in this manner befit your position as a ruler? Please take me back to my mother immediately. I shall then forget that you brought me forcibly here. I am the daughter of Jagabandhu Pattnaik, the landlord of the village Panchagada. You can send a mediator to my father if you intend to marry me. I would gladly serve the one as a maid to whom my father gives me away in marriage. But if anyone, be he the emperor of the world, holds me by force, without my father's permission, I shall consider him my enemy. My throat is parched with thirst. Please get me some water to drink."

The young man ordered his companion to get some water from the village nearby. He left immediately.

In the heart of the young man, who was devoid of all sense of morality and possessed with a sinful desire, there flamed an erotic passion at the touch of Padmamali. Now, left alone with her, the desire grew intenser. He slowly held the fingers of her small hands, which were lovely like champak buds and started in a humble voice:

"O, beautiful one, the arrow of the glance, shot off your lovely eyes, has pierced my heart. Don't be cruel to me any more. Take mercy on me or else I shall lay my life down at your feet. Say just for once that you will not disappoint me."

Padmamali: I have already told you that only my father will decide who I would marry. So you should not speak any more about this.

Saying so she pulled her hands out of his hold.

The young man: I believe that the landlord will not consider it beneath him to have me as his son-in-law. But before sending this proposal through a mediator, I would be extremely happy and consider myself fortunate if I can be sure that I have won the favour of his daughter.

Padmamali could not think up a quick reply to this. She was a very young girl and the idea of love had not yet found its way into the depths of her heart. She was yet to understand what love meant. Feeling or expressing her love for her abductor was out of question. Rather she took him to be her archenemy and was anxious to get rid of him as anyone would want to keep away from things that are vile and obnoxious. She analysed her present condition; she reasoned that if she showed any interest in him, using false words of endearment, the young man, taking advantage of her helplessness, might try to apply force and she would have to yield to him. On the other hand, if she rebuffed or rejected him, he might get provoked. Caught in such a vicious dilemma, she prayed Lord Vaidyanath (for whose worship she had kept the fasting today) and Goddess Mangala to save her and promised that if she escaped the danger, she would offer worship to the goddess. She begged the Lord, the saviour of the woe-stricken to come to her rescue. And, gathering all her courage, she said boldly:

"I regret to say that my answer will not be such as you have expected. What is the harm in speaking the truth? Your conduct was such that I can never bring myself to like you."

Her reply made him a little upset. He thought:

"If she does not favour me, her father would never give consent to our marriage. I have begged her in so many ways but she did not relent. What !!! -- Duryodhana Das, the mention of whose very name makes the whole kingdom of Nilagiri tremble in fear, will stand insult and humiliation from the daughter of an ordinary subject? Every woman in Nilagiri state yearns just for a look of favour from me. The same Duryodhana Das has now put his prestige and position at stake. Throwing myself at her feet, I have offered to be her slave and she has turned down my request! It can never be! Had she agreed to accept my love, she would have enjoyed the honour that befits the queen of Nilagiri. Since she has rejected me and behaved in this manner, I shall keep her as a concubine to gratify my lust. Now she is in my hands. Once she is deprived of her chastity, she would submit herself to me forever."

Analysing the situation thus, Duryodhana Das (there is no need to call him the young man anymore) said:

"Look, I am Duryodhana Das. There is no woman in Nilagiri who does not crave my favour. I had thrown myself at your feet and begged for your love. Had you fulfilled my desire, you would have enjoyed the luxury to which the queen of Nilagiri is entitled, but you did not oblige me. Rather your behaviour has aroused my anger. I have managed to get hold of you, be it through strategy or through coercion. I must fulfill my desire. Let's see who is going to stop me !"

Uttering these words, Duryodhana attempted to lift Padmamali to his lap by force. The helpless girl, scared out of her wits, screamed loudly, calling out to her mother.

The reader might remember that in the temple premises while Duryodhana and his companion Balabantaray were conspiring to abduct Padmamali, the shadow of a man had flitted across them and dissolved in the darkness. The person, whose shadow it was, had eavesdropped on their conversation and had come to know of the evil intentions of the criminals. He had kept close to them like a shadow, unnoticed. He had stealthily followed Duryodhana and was closely watching his activities standing at a distance under a mango tree. When Padmamali screamed, he thought that the ruffian was harassing her and came out of his hiding place. Moving at the speed of lightning, he appeared in front of Duryodhana and without wasting any time, released Padmamali's hands from Duryodhana's grip. Duryodhana shouted, his body trembling in rage:

"Who are you? How dare you risk my ire.?"

The newcomer: I am the saviour ·of the helpless and the distressed.

Duryodhana: Well, let's see, how you will save this girl?

Saying this, Duryodhana landed a blow on the newcomer. The newcomer had no intention of attacking Duryodhana unless he gave him a cause. Since Duryodhana provoked him by dealing the first blow, he grabbed Duryodhana's waist in his strong muscular arms and both of them were immediately engaged in a fierce scuffle. They were evenly matched in agility and strength. After they wrestled for some time, the newcomer laid Duryodhana flat on the ground and pounced upon him like a lion. Planting his own thigh over his chest and gripping his neck with his hand, he kept Duryodhana pinned to the ground. Immobilising Duryodhana in this manner, he made a sound as if signalling someone. A third man arrived immediately. With his associate's help, the newcomer fastened Duryodhana's hands at his back tightly with his stoll and tied him to the trunk of an old banyan tree that stood nearby. "Devil !" he said, "Suffer the consequences of your wickedness."

"Duryodhana Das will certainly avenge this one day,"

Duryodhana hissed, impotent like a venomless python.

Without paying heed to the boastful bravado, the newcomer went along with his associate to the place where Padmamali lay.

Chapter III

The Awakening of Love

The stranger found Padmamali trembling like a plantain tree in a storm. He assured her that she was safe now and that she had nothing to fear.

Human heart has strange ways. While it gets easily drawn towards some people, it feels repelled by others. In case of Duryodhana the latter quality had revealed itself. But at the sight of the stranger the opposite feelings took over her. Padmamali had never seen him before nor had she exchanged a word with him; in spite of this her heart was automatically drawn towards him even before he consoled her and she became sure that the person was her well wisher and no harm was to be expected from him.

I am unable to explain why people react this way. The learned readers having access to human psychology may investigate the matter. But if I distort the truth, I shall not be doing my duty. I am narrating here exactly what had happened.

Assured by the stranger of her safety, Padmamali said:

"O, noble one, you must be a god; taking mercy on me you have alighted from the heavens to save me from this danger. It is true that my parents have given me birth, but you have made me permanently indebted to you by rescuing me from this villain. I shall never be able to repay your debt."

Readers may feel surprised at such a reply from a sixteen-year-old girl. In order to remove their doubts, I must therefore say a few things about Padmamali. She was the only child of Jagabandhu Pattnaik, who was quite well to do. That he was only a landlord of Panchagada and the annual revenue income of that village did not amount to much should not make the readers presume that his position and prestige were that of an ordinary village chief. He lived in his ancestral house. He had inherited wealth that was acquired over generations. This included zamindaries and vast stretches of rent-free lands, and many estates. Padmamali was the only child of such a wealthy father. Before she was ten, Padmamali had read a good number of books such as. *Koyili,Gopibhasha, Rahasha* and the *Bhagabat*. At the special request of Purushottama Vidyaratna, the family priest of Jagabandhu Pattnaik, who had noticed the intelligence of Padmamali, her father had made her read many lyrics and plays and books such as *Kaumudi* and *Amara*. Besides these, she had also gone through classics like: *Labanyabati, Rasha Kallola, Prema Sudhanidhi* and *Vidagdha Chintamani*. Jagabandhu Pattnaik used to take pride in Padmamali's ability to understand and appreciate these literary texts.

Listening to Padmamali the stranger was even more astonished than our readers. He had not expected from a girl as young as Padmamali such felicity of language and clarity of thought. He replied:

"Having heard you, I am unable to decide whether it is your a beauty or your intelligence that is more praiseworthy. I have taken a vow to perform the sacred duty of serving the distressed and punishing the wicked. Helping in this small way a beautiful and intelligent lady like you, I have fulfilled my vow. It is quite late in the night; a shelter is available not far away from here. Tonight you will rest there; early in the morning we shall send a message to your mother."

Padmamali: My respect for you grows as I observe the nobility and unselfishness of your character. But I feel ashamed when you address me so respectfully. My name is Padmamali. I shall be glad if you address me by my name. I am ready to go whatever place you will take me to; because l know that I have nothing to be afraid of as long as I am under your protection.

Stranger: All right, as you wish, I shall address you as Padmamali. There is a place nearby where we can take shelter. Let's spend the night there. The road is impassable and the night is pitch dark. You must hold my hand for support.

Without hesitation Padmamali took the stranger's hand into her.

How astonishing! The touch sent a strange shiver through their bodies as if they had been pricked with the sharp points of countless needles. Is there an electric force lying dormant in the human body that got released by this contact and generated the current? Let our scientist readers explain it,

The bodies of both bristled with an excitement never experienced before and both of them felt ecstatic. But neither of them spoke about it and walked down the road in silence.

Chapter IV

The Monastery

The trio walked for about twelve minutes and reached a temple. They climbed a flight of steps and came up to a door. A servant opened the door at their knocking. Seeing the young man, he put down the lamp he was carrying and bowed, touching his head to the ground.

"Has the Mahanta gone to bed?" The stranger enquired.

"No Sir" the servant said. He led the way, lamp in hand. Padmamali, the young man and his associate followed him. They crossed a large courtyard and arrived at the bedroom of the Mahanta. The house was a two-storied wooden building. The valet went inside to announce the arrival of the guests. The Mahanta ordered him to usher the guests in immediately. The young man and Padmamali climbed a flight of wooden steps and entered the bedroom.

The bedroom measured about seven yards in length and five yards in width. There was a small adjoining room. The Mahanta sat on a string bed. A wooden bedstead stood facing him. Padmamali and the young man greeted him bowing their heads. The young man narrated the incidents that had taken place in detail. Their clothes were wet through. The Mahanta ordered his valet to provide the guests with new silk clothes and bring some sweetmeats for them.

After they changed into dry clothes and had their meals, a bed was laid out for Padmamali in the adjoining room. She lay down on the bed. Whether she went to sleep or not we shall find out later.

Having finished his meal, the young man came to sit on the bedstead.

The Mahanta asked: So, the girl is Jagabandhu Pattnaik's daughter?

"Yes. He is the landlord of Panchagada village," the young man answered.

Mahanta: I know him quite well. He is the son of Niladri Pattnaik. He frequently visited us while I was in Balasore. I too used to visit Panchagada occasionally. Jagu was a young boy at that time. I see, she is the daughter of that same Jagu. She is beautiful.

Young man: She is more intelligent than beautiful."

Mahanta: (Jestfully) What? In such a short time you have started to speak in her favour?

Young man: You may find it funny, but you can verify the truth after you talk to her.

Mahanta: Well, we shall see to that. So, it was Duryodhana Das who had abducted her. It has also come to my notice that the villain has kept the kingdom of Nilagiri under his despotic control. The dignity, prestige and property of the people are not safe and secure there.

Young man: In that case he will not desist from harassing Padmamali in future.

Mahanta: (to himself) It seems, this young fellow has come under the spell of beauty. (Aloud) He may not be able to bring any harm to her. I cannot believe that he will dare trouble the grand daughter of Niladri Pattnaik. Moreover, Panchagada is quite close to Balasore. I have heard that a magistrate named Sir Ricketts is now in charge of Balasore. He is a good administrator and is quite concerned about the well being of the subjects. It is not likely that Duryodhana Das will be able to harm anybody belonging to a place not far from the area under his jurisdiction.

Young man: That may be true. But had I known all this about him before, I would have kept him a captive instead of leaving him tied to the tree.

Mahanta: There is no need to worry. He can do her no harm.

Young man: Total anarchy prevails in Nilagiri now. Queen Chitra Devi orders the affairs of the state as the guardian of the minor prince. Haribabu says that the people there are passing through a bad time.

Mahanta: This state of affairs will not continue for long. Too much of any thing is bad. Duryodhana Das, through his action and his behaviour, is heading fast towards his downfall.

Young man: Perhaps it would be better if we bring the matter to the notice of the sahib in Balasore and ask him to set things right. Why don't you meet him once and bring everything to his knowledge?

Mahanta: Yes; I intend to go Balasore one of these days. I shall meet him then.

Both Mahanta and the young man went to sleep while talking about these matters.

Chapter V

The Love Bug

Padmamali had never seen the young man before nor had he for his part taken good look at her during their short meeting in the darkness of the night. In the faint light of the lamp in Mahanta's bedroom, their eyes fell on each other. They both were amazed. Neither of them could be sure whether the experience was real or one out of dream. The young man had never thought that such beauty could be found anywhere in this world. He marveled at the discovery. Padmamali looked at the young man and wondered if Kandarpa, the god of love, had descended on the earth assuming a human form. In short, both of them fell in love at first sight.

The young man was around twenty-one years of age. His fair face glowed with a rare radiance. The beauty of his eyes, large and slightly tinged in red, was enhanced by the rainbow shaped curve of his brows placed just in the middle of a broad forehead. The expression in his eyes reflected a mature mind. The soft hair of his moustache and his beard, instead of marring the loveliness of his face, added to it. He was finely dressed. His looks and his attire indicated his noble descent.

As they entered the Mahanta's retiring room, he asked them to take their seats. Padmamali looked at the young man and was reluctant to sit beside him. But the Mahanta took her by the hand and made her sit near him. She could not protest and sat there, her head lowered bashfully. Her face looked even more beautiful when she blushed and bent it down. The young man was not able to take his eyes off her face. Padmamali, raising her face, glanced at him and their eyes met; it was as if the beams from their eyes converged into one ray of light and their hearts started beating fast in unison.

Let the people interested in discovering scientific truths determine in what manner this reaction is related to the external world. But we know, as their eyes met, their hearts submerged in the surging waves of love.

Watching them the old Mahanta thought that the Supreme Creator had made them for each other, to add to each other's joy. If anyone of this pair was placed apart from the other, he thought, our eyes would be deprived of witnessing a sight which is beautiful beyond imagination. Whether anyone else observed it or not the sight of the couple delighted the old man.

Having listened to the incident relating to the abduction of Padmamali from the young man, Mahanta said, "I can't blame Duryodhana if he felt tempted to win this girl. Had I not been old I might have stolen her as Duryodhana did."

Hearing such words from the old man Padmamali blushed and sat there her eyes downcast. The Mahanta ordered his servants to treat the guests properly. A companion-maid was employed to attend to Padmamali. The companion-maid guided Padmamali to an adjoining room. A bed was laid there for her. She removed her wet clothes, changed into a new silk saree and after eating a little sweetmeat went to bed. She stretched herself on the bed and rested. But she could not sleep.

She brooded over the incidents that had come to pass during the past one hour –Duryodhana kidnapping her and the young man coming to her rescue, her repulsing Duryodhana and her getting drawn to the young man. She admitted to herself that the young man had done her a great service. It is natural that the heart is easily drawn towards the one who helps you. The young man had won her heart even before she saw him properly in the light of the lamp and when she set her eyes on his attractive figure, the love bug bored its way to the deepest recesses of her heart.

The young man too was enthralled and flicked several furtive glances at her. Suddenly, when their eyes met neither of them wished to turn them away from each other.

Do eyes speak? As far as we know, both of them exchanged their feelings through their eyes. The girl guessed that the young man looked at her with loving eyes, and he could understand that the girl's heart was not bereft of love for him. They stole each other's heart. I can't surmise how they would have reacted had there not been a third person around; the old Mahanta was there. Their eyes remained locked for a brief moment, then Padmamali blushed and turned her face away. The young man too looked in the other direction. The old Mahanta noticed all these. But they were not aware of it.

A wooden partition separated her room from that of the Mahanta. She overheard everything that passed between the young man and the Mahanta. From what she heard, she was certain that the young man wished well of her. A few hours before she was but a small girl, but in the course of these few hours she got transformed into a thoughtful young woman. She could not sleep and kept turning on her sides. The clever maid observed her restlessness and thought that she was exhausted because of the long walk. She started to massage Padmamali's feet although the later forbade her to do so.

It will be in order here to introduce the maid. Her name was Jayanti. She was the only child of the Gadanayak of Ghantashila. Although she was not exceptionally beautiful like Padmamali, she was not entirely devoid of charm. She was a little plump and her complexion had a dusky translucence. ·

Banchhanidhi Balabantaray, whom we have already met, was quite well known to Jayanti. She was the daughter of his maternal aunt's sister-in-law. They used to meet each other in her house since their childhood. As they grew older, the childhood friendship deepened into a deep love for each other. Balabantaray's aunt had no objection to their marriage. But there was something else that created a problem: Jayanti's father had promised to give his daughter in marriage to the son of the Dalabehera of Srirampur. Even the date of marriage had been fixed. Broken-hearted, Jayanti spent her days in great agony. The old Mahanta, having heard all this and hoping that a change of place might benefit her and that the passage of time would mitigate her grief, had brought her over to the monastery.

While she continued to massage gently, the feet of Padmamali, Jayanti said: Dei (sister), you went through a lot of pain.

Padmamali: I had been in a great danger. Rescuing me from that danger, the young man had made me permanently indebted to him.

Jayanti: All this is the work of providence; had it

not been so, you two could not have met easily. Let God Almighty fulfill your wish soon.

Padmamali: Will that ever be possible?

Jayanti : Why not?

Padmamali: (Sighing deeply) Can't you guess? It is obvious from his looks and manners that he is some powerful prince. Do you know him?

Jayanti: No sister. I am seeing him for the first time.

Padmamali: He is definitely not the Routray Prithviraj Bhanja, because I have seen the Routray at Mantri.

Jayanti: Who must he be?

Padmamali: Whoever he may be --- to aspire to marry him is as futile as a child stretching out its hands to catch the moon.

Jayanti: Why do you give up hope? You would not have felt so frustrated had you heard his conversation with the Mahanta.

Padmamali: (Keeping quiet for some time) Jayanti, have you ever fallen in love with someone? Then you can understand to some extent how I suffer.

Jayanti: Sister, you do not have any idea of the agony I have gone through. It has corroded my heart.

Padmamali was so eager to know the story of Jayanti's suffering that the later had to narrate the sad story of her life in detail. The night advanced as they continued talking. Both tried to sleep. Padmamali fell asleep for her journey had worn her out. But the image Padmamali's waking heart dwelt upon was not erased from the canvas of her mind even in her sleep. The young man appeared in her dream. She dreamt that she strolled with him in a beautiful garden. The green loveliness of the surrounding woods charmed their eyes; the air, heavy with the exotic fragrance of the wild jasmines pleased their nostrils. Gentle wafts of the cool south wind caressed them and soothed their bodies. The young man spoke honeyed words of love into her ears and the inmost core of her heart was filled with an exquisite happiness. The joy that surged within her was in perfect harmony with the joy with which the air vibrated. As she basked in the happiness within and the joy around, the sky suddenly became overcast. The forest that fascinated the eyes, turned fierce. The gentle breeze changed into violent gusts of wind that blew the fragrance of the forest flowers away. And the fearsome figure of Duryodhana loomed large across the sky.

Padmamali screamed. Her scream woke up Jayanti, who was sleeping by her bedside. She guessed that Padmamali had a bad dream and, coming to her, she placed her hands on Padmamali.

Padmamali opened her eyes. The maid asked, "Sister, were you frightened?"

"Yes, it was a bad dream that terrified me" Padmamali answered.

Jayanti; Dreams are unreal; you need not fear them.

Padmamali did not say anything. She looked at the fading glow of the lamp light and asked:

'Is it morning?'

"Yes, sister." Jayanti replied.

"Let us get up, then," Padmamali suggested.

They got up from their beds and walked into the garden outside.

Chapter VI

The Lovers Meet

The retiring-quarter of the Mahanta was spread in the north-south direction. The chamber in the south served as Mahanta's bedroom, and the one to the north was used to store valuables. Padmamali spent the night in this room. Close to the retiring quarters, towards its east, lay about five acres of land, where seasonal vegetables like the brinjals, bananas and potatoes were grown. Foreign vegetables like cauliflower and cabbages, turnips and peas were rare in the country those days. At the end of the garden, there lay a medium-sized, square tank full of clean fresh water, with coconut trees skirted around it. On the north side of the tank, a row of stone-steps led in to the water. Padmamali went through her bathing in this tank. After she finished, she wished to spend some time in the solitude of the garden and her companion-maid returned to the house.

To the north, east and south of the pond orchards of mango and jack-fruit were spread out. Next to it, an extensive forest of sal, teak and palm trees reached up to the valley of a small mountain.

After she strolled for some time, Padmamali sat down on a smooth boulder, under a leafy bakula tree. A 'madhavi' creeper which entwined itself around the tree, filled the air with its sweet fragrance.

Padmamali's golden skin, rubbed with saffron and freshly bathed, was draped in a blue saree. Her loose thick black hair, massaged with scented oil, cascaded down her back, sending waves of exotic fragrance into the air around.

She was very thoughtful and her lotus-like face looked serious. Her large eyes were calm. The soft morning breeze made a lock of hair dance wantonly on her lovely forehead.

She wore a few ornaments; she was not interested in them. Nature had made her so beautiful that jewellery helped but a little to enhance her charm. There were gem-studded wrist-lets aound her hands, a gold chain and necklace studded with diamond and sapphire adorned her neck. On her nose she wore a peacock shaped diamond nose-stud. A diamond ring circled her ring finger and a waistband of gold hung loosely around her buttocks. These ornaments added to the beauty of her figure.

It was not easy to fathom what passed in Padmamali's mind, but she gazed steadily at the beauty of the rising sun. The light of the rising sun made the gems in her ornaments glitter.

The young man woke up. He sent a messenger to Padmamali's mother. After discharging this duty, he bathed in the tank in the garden. He was charmed by the natural beauty of the place and wandered about.

We, human beings, are slaves to destiny. We are dragged by circumstances along the course that is already charted for us. Though we are unaware of it, our actions carry out the decree of Providence. The young man wandering aimlessly here and there reached the bakula tree under which Padmamali was sitting. Standing a short distance away, he watched her. The cords of his heart quivered seeing Padmamali, looking like some sylvan goddess in that morning hour. The thirst in his eyes was not quenched though he watched her lovely face for a very long time. The more he beheld her, the keener the thirst grew. There is no further need to tell the readers that the young man was completely bewitched with the beauty and virtue of the girl.

He could not hold back the temptation to speak to her when he found her alone. He walked slowly towards her.

Padmamali watched the rising sun in rapt attention. She was not aware of his presence. She looked at the sun for a long time and prayed softly: "O' God, you make day and night follow each other; you mow our sorrows. Last night I was saved from Duryodhana. But why is my heart getting drawn towards the person who saved me? His looks and his deportment clearly indicate that he must be some prince in disguise. O' God, you bear witness to the fact that I am not doing this willingly. I leave everything in your hands." Praying thus, she touched her folded hands to her forehead in reverence.

Did the Sun God grant her prayers!

When she turned and discovered the very person whose image she had been meditating upon standing before her, she was certain that the young man had heard her prayer and felt deeply embarrassed.

The heart of a woman is made up of strange stuff. When the person, whose thought had filled her heart, appeared before her, Padmamali blushed and got up to leave the place.

"Padmamali," the young man called, "you are leaving the place as soon as you have seen me."

She stopped. As she recollected how deeply she was indebted to him, her feet refused to move. She sat down on the stone-seat that she had abandoned and hung her head down, blushing. Her face now radiated a loveliness that the young man had never seen before. His eyes feasted on this indescribable beauty, like a famine-stricken man devouring dishes placed before him. The loveliness that his eyes devoured also filled his other sense organ with joy.

Young Man: Padmamali, I was looking for an opportunity to speak to you--to tell you what deep love I feel in my heart for you. Luck has granted me this chance.

Padmamali: You are probably some prince in disguise. I am the daughter of an ordinary person. The union of the great and the humble ones is not desirable because in most cases such an uneven match makes the humble one suffer. Therefore, if love has awakened in your heart for me, I pray to you to refrain from pursuing it further.

Young Man: I am so enthralled by you that without you my life will be a meaningless void. My identity will be revealed to you in course of time. If you refuse to respond to my love, I shall never find happiness in this life. Let me assure you, my position and title will not pose impediments in the way of our union.

These words pleased her, but she said nothing. The young man took her silence for her consent. He came and sat down beside her. Again their bodies touched each other. The experience made them shiver with a divine ecstasy. The young man took Padmamali's hands in his own and gently touched her fingers, lovely as champak buds and said:

"Finding myself worthy of the love of such a beautiful and intelligent girl like you, I consider myself most fortunate. As long as there is life in my body, the sole object of my life will be to make you happy in all possible ways."

Padmamali: I offer myself at your feet, as your servant maid.

Young man: "No. Not a servant-maid. From now on you are the goddess of my heart."

Saying so, the young man lifted Padmamali to his lap and gazed at her face, which was beautiful like a lotus flower, with hungry eyes.

The wise readers should take account of the time, the solitude of the place and the fervour in the hearts of the lovers; you cannot blame the young lover when he planted a kiss on the red berry-like lips of the girl and enjoyed the bliss of love.

A few moments later, the young man said: "Padmamali; l shall take steps to make you mine forever; as soon as possible. The Mahanta's reaction clearly indicates his willingness to help us. Your father will not reject the Mahanta's proposal. I believe that our wish is going to be fulfilled soon. Till we meet again, wear this diamond ring as a memento" Saying so, the young man took out a precious diamond ring from his finger and slid it down the ring finger of Padmamali's right hand.

Padmamali, too, removed an expensive ring from her own finger and slid it down one of the fingers of the young man. "I shall be obliged if this ordinary ring brings me to your mind occasionally," she said.

After this, the lovers took to different paths and arrived at the Mahanta's place.

Chapter VII

Mahanta Harihara Ramanuja Das

In this short narrative, Mahanta Harihara Ranianuja Das has a major role to play. The need of furnishing the readers with a detailed introduction of the Mahanta cannot therefore be overlooked.

The Mahanta was a Maharastrian Brahmin. His name was Bajirao Sahib. When the kingdom of Utkal was under the rule of the Marathas, Bajirao Sahib served as the deputy of the collector of Balasore. In the year 1803, on receipt of orders issued by King Raghuji Bhonsle from the court of Nagpur, Bajirao Sahib handed over the charge of the estate to the British officers, Gen. Hirkutch and Sir Melville and retired from his job. But he did not go back to his native place. After the death of his wife and his only son, he had developed a feeling of detachment towards this world. He did not want to return to his native, place for this reason.

He was fairly old by the time he gave up his royal office. Though the court of Nagpur offered some other post to him, the Mahanta had decided to spend the rest of his life in Balasore. This was how, after the British took over the control of the state, Bajirao continued to live in Balasore.

In 1812, when the Queen of Mayurbhanja, Sumitra

Devi, passed away, Trivikram Bhanja Deo was made the king of Mayurbhanja. The Mahanta had taken special interest in the matter and saw to it that Trivikram Bhanja Deo ascended the throne. After Trivikram Bhanja Deo was coroneted as the king, he put Bajirao Sahib in charge of Mayurbhanja fort, as a token of appreciation of the services he had rendered.

Bajirao Sahib gave up his native religion 'Ganapataya', which prescribed the worship of Lord Ganapathi and embraced 'Vaishnavism'. He was renamed 'Mahanta Harihara Ramanuja Das' and lived in the fort of Mayurbhanja.

The temple and the monastery, mentioned earlier, were constructed under the supervision of Maharaja Trivikram Bhanja Deo. After the Mahanta was placed in charge of the monastery, he was able to win the love and respect of the people in a very short time through his philanthropic and charitable acts. People from nearby villages gathered on the platform of Mahanta's monastery every evening. Disputes between villagers were placed before him for adjudication. His judgment was final. The firm faith which the villagers had in the Mahanta's impartiality made both complainants as well as respondents accept his decision without any objection. The decisions of the Mahanta were never appealed against.

Grand ceremonies were arranged in the monastery on festive occasions. Since the Mahanta had saved enough money during the period of Maratha rule, he spent the money on such occasions.

Though he had retired from his royal office, the Mahanta in a way had become something of a king ruling the nearby villages, and the people lived happily under his rule.

During the period in which this narrative has been set, the young folk, unlike their modern counterparts, had no knowledge of English and therefore they had not learnt to forsake moral conduct and decorum of behaviour. They did not arrogantly denounce their forefathers as 'stupid'. At that time modern principles and theories were not in vogue and people were orthodox in their outlook on life.

The connotations of terms like 'orthodox' and 'conservative' have changed these days. They are now used as derogatory adjectives to disparage the man who is called so. People in those days used to live in ill-ventilated houses, without proper light and air. But in modern times, we are afraid that such unhygienic lifestyle would harm us. But we have to admit, with reluctance may be, that our so called orthodox ancestors living in the ill-ventilated and dingy houses enjoyed a longer and healthier life of which we have been deprived despite the fact that we live in well-ventilated houses which, since they are regularly whitewashed, sparkle like snow.

The Mahanta was nearly eighty years old. But he never needed the assistance of Solomon & Co. glass company (it had not established its business in India then) to improve the sharpness of his eyesight. Nor did he need some American dentist to take care of his teeth to help digest food better.

He was a fair complexioned man. Though he was past eighty, there were no wrinkles on his skin. It would be enough to say that his glowing skin was as glossy and smooth as that of a ripe mango.

Returning from the garden, the young man found the Mahanta offering prayer to the Lord. The mother of Padmamali arrived at the monastery at about the same time. Such was the joy of both the mother and her daughter when they met that any description we might attempt would appear as an exaggeration. The guests halted for three more days in the monastery at Mahanta's request and the lovers got a number of opportunities to meet each other. In the early morning of the fourth day, they set off for their respective destinations. At the young man's order ten armed guards escorted Padmamali and her mother to their village.

Chapter VIII

The Retribution

Tied to the tree, Duryodhana Das felt utterly miserable. A few moments after Padmamali and the young man had left the place, Banchhanidhi Balabantaray arrived there carrying a jug of water. He was surprised when he did not find Duryodhana and Padmamali at the place where he had left them sitting. He sat down on the spot waiting for them to return. When, after a long wait, no one came, he started looking around for them. As he wandered here and there, a faint voice that sounded like Duryodhana's reached his ears. He pricked his ears and listened intently to find the direction from which the sound came.

Duryodhana, writhing in excessive pain, was calling out loudly the name of Balabantaray time and again and was showering abuses on him and his ancestors for his delay in returning from the village. Hours of grief and misery do not pass as quickly as those of joy. Duryodhana's agony grew in proportion to the delay in the return of Balabantaray. The first time when Duryodhana called out his name, Balabantaray' tried to listen carefully, but he could not be sure of the direction from which it was coming. When Duryodhana called out for the second time, Balabantaray could not hear it clearly as the sound of a thunderclap drowned it. Balabantaray got confused. He thought that the first sound that he had heard was only his imagination and instead of going towards the place where Duryodhana lay tied up, he walked in the opposite one. After spending a long time in a futile search, Balabantaray concluded that Duryodhana might have had left the place without waiting for him to return.

He went back to the village to return the jug. Imagine what thoughts must have crossed his mind as he overheard the following conversation between the master of the house and one of his friends. The friend told:

"Haven't you heard this? When the rain spoiled the fair, some wicked men, taking advantage of the confusion, snatched away a very beautiful girl."

"Really? Is this true?"

"Yes, the girl's mother went weeping to the tent of the Routray to make a complaint. The Routray sent his soldiers with torches to look for the girl. But the girl could not be traced, despite a thorough search."

"No ordinary man will venture to do a thing like this."

"All that could be found out was that Duryodhana Das of Nilagiri was following her. Nobody knew where he is. His own friends are looking for him. He is a notorious character. The possibility of Duryodhana being behind this abduction cannot be ruled out."

"What further steps did the Routray take, then?"

"He has sent a cavalry troop of eight soldiers to guard the roads leading to Kansari and Kaptipada. I suppose by this time they must have captured him and brought him to the Routray."

"It would not have been possible for Duryodhana

to kidnap a girl from the crowd single-handedly. He must have been helped by an accomplice."

Nidhi Balabantatay, a man of immense courage, was listening to all this from the beginning in intense anxiety. He could now understand why he did not find Duryodhana in the place where he should have been. His courage failed him when his own name was mentioned. He was so overcome with fear that the jug he held slipped off his hand hitting the floor with a loud clang. Startled with the sound, the master of the house and his friend hurried outside carrying the lamp and saw Balabantaray standing there, still as a puppet. He was not aware that the water jug had fallen. The master of the house seeing him in that condition guessed that he must have been frightened for some reason and took him inside. He offered him some food and drinks and requested him to spend the night in his house. Balabantaray did as he was told. He slept there and waking up very early in the morning, took leave from the master of the household and walked along the Kansari Street.

The morning was exquisitely beautiful during those early hours. Bathed in last night's shower, the trees and even the grass looked lush green. The warbles of birds like cuckoos, doves and bulbuls, poured music as sweet as ambrosia in his ears. The gentle morning breeze fanned his body and cooled it. His spirit lifted as he witnessed the loveliness of the landscape and he walked on humming a tune.

Reaching the place where Duryodhana and Padmamali had rested last night, he stood for a while and looked around. He could trace the marks of horse-hooves on the path. But he could not see those marks returning in the opposite direction. Had they returned, he would have been sure that Duryodhana Das had been captured. But now he was not so sure. He walked on feeling confused. Suddenly he came across something resembling the figure of a man. It did not lie sprawled on the ground in sleep, nor was it sitting upright. Balabantaray approached the figure and saw that it was no one but Duryodhana himself. Without wasting a moment Balabantaray untied him. Duryodhana's eyes were closed out of exhaustion but he was not asleep. He rose to his feet when Balabantaray unfastened him. But the unbearable agony he had gone through during the previous hours was not erased from his memory. As he analysed the events of the night before in order of their occurrence, he became certain that it was Balabantaray's not carrying out a proper search that had made him suffer so much. As soon as he arrived at this conclusion, it was impossible for him to control the upsurge of anger. Without saying a word he landed two heavy blows with his fist on the back of poor Balabantaray. The latter could not think of any reason for which so harsh a punishment was meted out to him; but he walked along the Kansan Street in silence and vowed to himself that one day he must avenge this humiliation.

Chapter IX

Hearsay

A few days passed by after the occurrence of the incidents narrated in the preceding chapters. One afternoon, Purushottama Senapati, the blacksmith, was working at his kiln. He was a resident of Panchagada and was Jagu Pattnaik's neighbour. He was the royal blacksmith of the kingdom of Nilagiri and was in receipt of sufficient land grant that made him a man of means.

Senapati lifted one after another piece of iron from the kiln with a pair of tongs and placed them on the anvil while one of his assistants hammered them into the required shapes. Another assistant kept blowing air into the kiln with the help of a blowpipe. At this time Banchhanidhi Balabantaray walked in slowly and sat down near Senapati. The memory of the incidents that had happened in Mayurbhanja made him very sad and depressed; he had chosen not to meet anyone on his return from Mayurbhanja for this reason. Senapati was fond of Balabantaray and used to offer him words of advice whenever he came to him. But today, he did not speak to him; he did not even turn his face to look at him. Balabantaray, unable to guess the reasons of such indifference, continued to sit in silence. After some time Senapati said: "Well, Balabantaray, you have made a grand display of gallantry at Mayurbhanja I understand."

Balabantaray became speechless. He was shocked that the report of what had transpired in the pitch dark of the night in Mayurbhanja had already reached Nilagiri. He felt as if the heavens above came crashing down over his head. He realised that Senapati had got to know everything and decided that it would not be wise to hide from him whatever he himself knew. At the same time, he wanted to ascertain how much Senapati knew.

He asked guardedly:

"What gallantry?"

"You are asking me? Everyone knows that Duryodhana is a rogue; but how could you get involved in the kidnapping of the landlord Jagu Pattnaik's daughter?" Senapati demanded.

Balabantaray had no idea that the girl was the landlord's daughter. He cursed himself when he learnt this and said:

"I was not aware that she was the landlord's daughter. Had I known, I would never have acted this way. I shall regret this as long as I live. Duryodhana asked me to fetch him water and I went away. I did not know what happened after that. I shall feel relieved if I could know that no harm had come to the daughter of the landlord,"

"No, she did not come to any harm. God saved her from Duryodhana."

"Please tell me. I am very anxious to know what happened."

"When Duryodhana found himself alone with her, he tried to win her over with sweet words of love, but she did not give in. Then he started applying force. But God always comes to the rescue of the weak. At that hour, Routray Prithvinath Bhanja arrived there and saved her."

"I see! Routray Babu did not rest just by sending his troops after Duryodhana; he himself came to capture him. When I went to the village to return the water jug, I heard there that the Routray had sent troops after Duryodhana."

"Yes, he himself went with them. After he released Padmamali, he made arrangement for her to spend the night in a monastery. He fetched her mother the next day and sent them home with escorts."

"Royal personages conduct themselves differently. Do you know what happened to Duryodhana after that?"

"No. Padmamali can't say anything about him."

"Serves the villain right. But he deserved more. He will definitely pay for this one day."

"How was he punished?"

"The penalty he paid was enough. Even then I am not satisfied."

"Why don't you say what punishment was meted out to him?" "After I came carrying a tumbler of the water; I did not find Duryodhana where I had left him."

"What did you do?"

"I searched and searched, but I did not find him anywhere." "What did you do after that?"

"I went back to return the water jug."

"What happened next?"

"Arriving at the house from ·where I had brought water, (the master of the house had taken so good care of me, poor man!) I heard someone from Mantri narrating the incident of Padmamali's abduction by Duryodhana, (Why blame Duryodhana? It was I who had snatched Padmamali). I learnt there that the Routray has sent his troops to track Duryodhana down. I was at my wit's end when I heard that. I was afraid that those people would recognise me. I was so scared that the jug slipped off my hands. They came to me when they heard the sound. When they asked me why I was so frightened, I lied that I saw a ghost clad in white under the banyan tree."

"You idiot! I asked you how Duryodhana was punished and what nonsense you are talking."

"How can I tell you of the end unless I begin at the beginning?"

"Well, go on."

"I slept that night in the village. I gathered from what I heard that the Routray had arrested Duryodhana. I returned in the morning. On the way I saw marks of horse-hooves. I noticed that those marks went in one direction, but there was no sign of the horses returning. I wondered about what had happened to Duryodhana when I could not find the marks of horse-hooves going in the opposite direction. Had they captured Duryodhana, they would have returned in the ditettion from which they came. I came to the place where Duryodhana had sat last night and looked around; then I noticed something at a distance looking like a human being."

"Was it Duryodhana?"

"Yes, it was."

"What was he doing there?"

"What else could he be doing? He could not even to move from that place."

"Why?"

" I found him tied to a tree, his back towards me."

" What !"

" I tell you the truth."

"Did he remain like that throughout the night?"

"He did. What else could he have done?"

"He must have suffered all night. What happened next?"

"There is no doubt that he did. As the villain had sown, so had he reaped."

"Who released him?"

"It was my ill luck that I did so."

"Why do-you say so?"

"When I got there, I found him sitting with his eyes closed. I felt scared when I found him in that condition and untied him. But the moment he was set free, the wicked fellow landed two heavy blows on my back."

"It is not wise to help the wicked even when you find him in trouble. But why did he hit you?"

"He alone knows why he did that. But I shall not rest until I settle the score."

As they talked, the sun went down in the west. Senapati stopped his work and prepared to go back home. But he asked his assistant, Pahala Gochhayat, not to tell anyone about what had passed between him and Balabantaray.

Chapter X

The News Spreads

Pahala Gochhayat went home. He ate his meal and stretched himself on the bed. But sleep did not come to his eyes that night. On other occasions, after dinner, as soon as he lay sprawled on the bed resting his head on the pillow, he fell asleep immediately. But tonight was an exception. When his wife, having finished her household chores, entered the bedroom, she found Pahala awake. Surprised, she remarked:

"Something very unusual has happened tonight!"

"What is it?"

"Every night when I enter the bedroom, I find you fast asleep. I am surprised to see you awake tonight."

Pahala tried to sound romantic and said: "I have been waiting to see your moon-like face."

"How fortunate I am to hear this', Mayana replied. 'How I yearn to listen to a few words of love from you, but every night when I come to the bedroom, I find you lost in deep slumber and I go to sleep with a heavy heart."

"Mayana, how happy I am to have a wife like you! Why didn't you tell me this before? From today onwards I shall never go to sleep until you come."

Poor Mayana's heart melted when she heard these words. She said: "You toil throughout the day; you require rest. It is good for your health; I never wish to disturb you while you rest. I feel happy if you are happy. My parents have stopped worrying after they have given me in marriage to you. I for my part have no complaints."

Pahala propped himself up on the bed and planted a kiss on Mayana's cheek the sound of which must have been heard even a mile away. She did not protest. He lay down again and Mayana started to massage his feet.

Pahala found it hard to digest the food he had consumed; his stomach churned. He realised that unless he divulged the secret he had kept concealed, he would suffer from indigestion. So he said:

"Dear, haven't you heard it?"

"What?"

"You wanted to go to Mantri; had you gone there, you would have met a terrible fate."

"Why? What would have happened to me? So many people went there. What terrible things happened to them?"

"They alone know what they went through."

"Tell me what they went through," Mayana asked.

"Padmamali was abducted by a villain."

"What are you saying! How was she rescued?"

"It was her good luck that she was saved ... Otherwise it would have been the end of the road for Jagu Pattnaik."

"Has the abductor been identified?"

"Yes, he has been found out, but I shall not tell who he was. You are a woman; you may not be able to keep it a secret."

Mayana sulked, thinking that her husband did not consider her trustworthy. Pahala noticed that his reluctance to confide m Mayana had hurt her. At the same time, he felt his stomach churn. He could not rest till he disclosed everything he knew.

He pulled Mayana on to his lap and said sweetly: "Why are you getting angry? Listen, I shall tell you everything."

"No, there is no need to. You have no faith in me." Mayana, remembering her parents, started to sob.

"I am sorry. It is my fault that I did not trust you. Don't take it to heart. Who else would abduct Padmamali? It was the brother of the Queen of your state, Duryodhana."

"What! Didn't he know that she was the landlord's daughter?"

"Due punishment was meted out to the villain."

"What punishment?"

"When the Routray came to know that Duryodhana had kidnapped her, he went after him with his soldiers. After travelling a long way, he finally tracked him down. While rescuing Padmamali from him, he had given him a good beating. His soldiers also joined him. Duryodhana had been so badly beaten that his entire body looked swollen like that of a frog. He lost consciousness. Then they fastened his hands at his back and tied him to a tree. He remained there like that all night."

"Who set him free?" Mayana asked.

"Who else? That stupid Balabantaray."

"Why did the idiot do that?" ·

"He also reaped the consequence of his foolishness."

"What consequence?"

"As soon as Duryodhana was untied, he gave Balabantaray two heavy blows."

"Serves him right."

"Yes, But, be careful, you must not disclose this to anyone. The wicked man may create trouble for us if he comes to know that you have."

The couple went to sleep. Early in the morning, Pahala went about his work and Mayana got busy attending to the household chores. But she could not concentrate her mind on anything. As it was with Pahala, something stirred inside her and she decided that she would not rest in peace until she brought it out.

She swept the floor, but could not continue for long and, broom in hand, she came to her mother-in-law. The old woman was busy brushing her teeth; seeing Mayana, she asked :

"What is the matter, daughter-in-law?"

"Haven't you heard anything?"

Having narrated the episode involving Duryodhana and Padamamali, which Pahala had told her in exaggerated details, she added:

"It was the landlord's good luck that Routray of the kingdom of Mayurbhanja followed Duryodhana on horseback on that dark night, captured him and rescued the girl. But who knows what he did after that? I ask you. Could Duryodhana have been able to abduct the girl without her consent? The girls of these days tend to force themselves on men; why should we blame only the men? I am confident that even if thousands of such Duryodhanas come they can't do this to me."

Mayana having unburdened herself in this manner went back to her household work. Her mother-in-law, finding that there was not much work left for her to do at that time, went to the house of her old friend, the mother of Jayakrishna Pattnaik, to have a chat.

Both the women were about the same age and were good friends. Pahala's mother proclaimed everywhere that there was no such person as good as Jayee's mother. Jayee's mother also expressed similar sentiments regarding her friend. She used to say that she had never seen (she was sixty) a person as good as the mother of Pahala.

When Jayee's mother saw her friend she asked:

"Well, Pahala Maa (Pahala's mother), it is a long time since you came here last."

"What can I say, dear sister! I don't find any time these days to visit you. My son remains out at work, throughout the day. The time has become such these days that it is not wise to leave a young daughter-in-law alone in the house and go out."

"Why? How have things changed these days?"

"Such incidents now occur in families of high social standing that we, the poor and the lowly, get worried about our own safety."

"What has occurred in what high class family?" Jayee's mother asked.

Pahala's mother now needed no further persuasion. Without any prelude, she repeated everything she had heard from her daughter-in-law. Of course she did not forget to add to the arrative her own comments from time to time. After she got to the end of her story, she repeatedly cautioned her friend not to reveal this matter to anyone else and walked back to her house.

Jamuna, the servant maid in Jayakrishna Pattnaik's house, eavesdropped while the two women were talking. She could not keep quiet when she heard it. She told all about it to Dama's mother, who was her good friend and warned her to keep the matter a secret. But as soon as Dama came for lunch, his mother narrated to him the story from the beginning to the end.

Dama heard this and hurried to the opium den to tell his friends about the incident. We have learnt from reliable sources that Dama took two extra doses of opium than his regular quota that day.

In the opium den there was a lot of discussion and argument over the topic that day; people present there relayed the story to their close acquaintances. And the news of Padmamali's abduction and the punishment inflicted on Duryodhana spread like wildfire in the town. Everywhere people were found talking about it.

Chapter XI

The History of Nilagiri

It seems necessary now to turn a few leaves of the history of Nilagiri before we take this narrative any further.

In 1832, Govinda Chandra Mardaraj, the king of Nilagiri, passed away, leaving behind his three widows and two minor sons. His youngest queen, the daughter of Madhusudan Pattnaik, had borne him these sons. Of these two, the elder one, prince Krishna Chandra Mardaraj Harichandan ruled over Nilagiri. He was not more than ten years of age at the time. During his minorship, the Commissioner of Orissa and the Superintendent of the Gadajat States placed the affairs of the state in the hands of the queen, Chitra Devi.

The queen was a young woman. She therefore appointed her brother Sivacharan Pattnaik as the Dewan to assist her in managing the affairs of the kingdom. The subjects of Nilagiri were so much oppressed under Siva Pattnaik's rule that most of them, along with the entire army, entered into a conspiracy with Harihara Bhramarabara (known as Hari Babu). There was total anarchy. When the conditions of lawlessness exceeded the limit, the Commissioner Sahib was compelled to pay a visit to Nilagiri. When he came, he found that there were not even ten soldiers in the state who pledged allegiance to the queen.

Hari Babu himself was an aspirant to the throne of Nilagiri. History does not furnish us with adequate information regarding the closeness of his relationship with the royal dynasty of Nilagiri. He had tried to usurp the throne of Nilagiri by filing a case in the court to establish his claim, and also even by force. But he could not succeed in either of his efforts. Earlier, his father Dasarathi Mangaraj had filed a case in the civil court claiming his rights over the throne of Nilagiri. But, later, he had withdrawn the case after receiving an allowance from Govinda Chandra Mardaraj. Hari Babu, too, had put his claim before the court and was granted an annual pension amounting to Rs.120 from the royal treasury of Nilagiri. However, this did not stop him from craving the throne. He had married the sister of the king of Kaptipada. With the aid of the king of Kaptipada and the Routray of Mayurbhanja, Prithvinath Bhanja, Hari Babu, with a troop of soldiers, launched sporadic attacks on Nilagiri, plundering the crops and the livestock that belonged to the subjects. As it was, the subjects of Nilagiri were passing through a troublesome time under the rule of Siva Pattnaik; and this tyranny of Hari Babu left them with no alternative but to seek his (Hari Babu's) protection.

Hari Babu did not stop at only harassing the subjects; he created so much trouble that the life of the young prince of Nilagiri came to be endangered. One night, the son of a traitor, Bhagawan Babu, broke into the palace with an intention to kill the minor prince. But he was captured before he succeeded in carrying out his evil designs. Such repeated threats to the life of the prince forced Queen Chitra Devi to take shelter in the house of Satrughna Pattnaik along with her two little sons. From there, she went to Balasore and sought the help of the magistrate. The magistrate, renowned for his benevolence, appointed a habildar as her bodyguard. He sent the queen back to the fort with her bodyguard and ten other attendants.

For the condition that prevailed in Nilagiri, of which an account is given earlier in this chapter, Duryodhana was responsible to a great extent. It has become necessary to introduce Duryodhana to the readers to enable them to examine if this claim is warranted.

Common people did not have a clear idea as to the parentage of Duryodhana. Madhusudan Pattnaik (the father of Queen Chitra Devi) had a sister named Ketaki. Madhusudan Pattnaik and his wife were very fond of her. She was beautiful. At sixteen, Pattnaik gave her in marriage to a man who was in the evening of his life and suffered from tuberculosis. The outcome of this uneven match was that Ketaki became a widow only six months after her marriage. The poor girl was plunged into the depths of eternal grief even before she experienced the pleasure of conjugal life. Her husband had a cousin named Ghanashyama, the son of his maternal uncle. Ghanashyama frequented the house of Ketaki's inlaws. At times, he stayed there for a few days. Since his relationship with Ketaki was that of a brother-in-law, she gradually opened up before him. She took the liberty of speaking to him in the presence of others. As days passed, she became bold enough to cut jokes and exchange jestful words with him.

After her husband's death, Ketaki bore the pangs of her widowhood for a few days. In course of time, the intensity of the anguish started to wear away. Meanwhile, Ghanashyama, taking advantage of Ketaki' s loneliness, made overtures to her. The loving words of Ghanashyama broke through the feeble wall of Ketaki's resistance and she drew closer to him. Eventually this liaison made her pregnant. As the pregnancy manifested itself, they tried to terminate the pregnancy but were unsuccessful.

At first Ketaki's sister-in-law noticed the symptoms of her pregnancy. Gradually her mother-in-law and the women in the neighbourhood came to know about it and started showering abuses on her day and night. Unable to bear the sting of such abuse, Ketaki, one night secretly left her in-laws' house and came to her parental home. That very night, she gave birth to Duryodhana and breathed her last. No one except Madhusudan Pattnaik, his wife and his mother knew about this.

Duryodhana was brought up in his maternal uncle's house. When he grew up, he worked along with Madhusudan Pattnaik's eldest son Siva Pattnaik. By dint of his cunning and craftiness, he took the reins of administration of Nilagiri into his own hands. Siva Pattnaik was Dewan only in name.

Duryodhana had not missed any opportunity to abuse the power he enjoyed. People's property and honour were not safe under Duryodhana's rule. A large number of the subjects, fed up with his tyranny, felt compelled to take sides with Hari Babu, forsaking their loyalty to the queen and the underage king.

Chapter XII

Duryodhana Conspires

Duryodhana returned to Nilagiri from Mayurbhanja. The humiliation he had suffered and the shame he had swallowed there burned like venom poured down his throat. He kept himself indoors for two or three days and refused to meet anyone, not even his friends and followers. He was yet to recover from the physical pain caused by the punishment that had been meted out to him at Mantri. He got up from the bed in the morning and after going through the routine works lay down again in bed. His mind remained constantly busy in finding a way to avenge the insult. He was in such a foul mood that even his valets were scared to go near him.

Valets usually let their masters know when people praise them or speak ill of them. On the third day of Duryodhana's return, his valet very cautiously informed him about the rumour that had spread in the town. Duryodhana seethed in rage when he heard it and ordered his valet to summon Laxmana Panda immediately. Laxmana Panda arrived without delay. He sat down on the floor. Those days in feudatory states subordinates considered it a privilege and not dishonour to sit on the floor before persons occupying positions of power.

Laxmana Panda was the head amin in the revenue department of the state of Nilagiri. He sath there for a while. After some time, turning on his side, Duryodhana asked:

"Is it Laxmana?"

" Yes Sir."

"What is the news?"

"Fine sir."

"You are making a casual remark. Is there nothing special?"

"No sir, nothing so special."

"Tell me."

"Whatever it is, it does not deserve your lordship's attention."

"Does not deserve my attention? If at all there is some special news, it is important that I should be told of it first."

"Yes, your lordship is right; but the special news I have heard….. it would be better if you don't listen to it."

"Why?"

"Sir, rumours never tell the truth. A tiny bit of truth multiplies hundredfold to become a rumour. These lies will annoy you and you will not be able to know who is responsible for spreading such rumour."

"You have increased my curiosity. Tell me; I am prepared to hear you calmly."

"Sir, people say that you took away the Patwari's daughter by force. The Routray caught you on the way and released the girl. After giving you a thorough beating he kept you tied to a tree. Wicked people are saying many other things in addition to this. You need not hear them."

Duryodhana remained silent for a while and said:

"Laxman, you are right, people always tend to exaggerate the truth."

"Sir, you know it better than me."

"Jagabandhu Pattnaik's daughter is beautiful like a heavenly nymph. When I came across her, I was seized with a desire to attain her. You know that I always get the object of my desire by hook or by crook. Unaware that she was the landlord's daughter and bewitched by her charms, I abducted her. But on the way I ran into a gang of robbers: they snatched the girl from me. This is the truth."

"I had never believed in the rumour. Now that you have let me know the truth, all doubts have disappeared from my mind. True, wretched people are capable of making a mountain out of a molehill."

"Let them do whatever they like," Duryodhana said, "time will expose their falsehood. One day they will see that the same Jagu Pattnaik's daughter, for whom such unpleasant things happened, will fall at my feet and beg for mercy. But at present you have to do something for me."

"This servant is at your lordship's disposal."

"You have to visit Panchagada at once."

"I will do so, sir."

"Tell the landlord that on that night, the fair at Mantri was spoiled by heavy downpour. The crowd, confused, ran here and there in search for shelter. I found his daughter alone and helpless there and brought her with an intention to keep her under my care. But, robbers attacked us on the way and unfortunately I could not save his daughter from them. Tell him that I am very glad to hear that his daughter had returned to him unharmed. Tell him also that having seen his daughter at Mantri I feel deeply interested in her and want to marry her. I shall be extremely pleased if the landlord grants my wish. This is the matter in brief.

Laxmana, you will go there with the proposal of marriage as the mediator from my side. Your persuasive ability will be put to test."

"Sir, it is a very small matter. Don't you worry. I shall leave for Panchagada very soon," Laxmana said.

Chapter XIII

The Sufferings of Padmamali

We have not met Padmamali for a long time. Readers, let us visit Panchagada to take a look at her.

That delicate maiden, whose beauty no words could describe, had visited Mantri prompted by a girlish curiosity but she had returned home as a thoughtful young woman. Padmamali was no longer her animated self. She looked serious and pensive; but why? Her father had property in abundance. If the use of rhetoric is permitted here, she was rolling in wealth. She was the only child of her parents. Was it that her stepping on the threshold of youth had made her so thoughtful? But there was no reason to be so. Because the man she loved had expressed his love for her in unequivocal words. Yet Padmamali visualised a number of obstacles in the way of their union. She had no doubt that he hailed from a royal family. An ordinary girl of the Mohanty family aspiring to marry a prince! What an absurdity!! The frightening image of Duryodhan she had seen in the dream in the night she spent at the monastery, kept haunting her. She considered Duryodhana as the most formidable adversary in the path of their marriage.

On one hand her heart was filled with a deep love for

the unknown young man and it was filled with misgivings in equal proportions on the other. She found herself caught in a vicious turmoil. She could have relieved herself of the burden that weighed heavy on her heart, had there been a close friend with her. She remembered Jayanti, whose presence could have helped to relieve her agony to a great extent. While, living in their parental homes; young unmarried girls are supposed to spend their time enjoying themselves. But Padmamali was now disinterested in all sorts of fun and merrymaking. She preferred to be alone and passed her days, lost in deep thoughts. And the result was obvious. As she neglected to take her food in time and lacked sleep, she fell sick. She ignored her sickness and it grew worse.

Eventually, Padmamali became bedridden. Gadadhar Tripathy, the village physician, remained by her side day and night and administered different kinds of drugs. But her condition did not show any signs of improvement. Some friends of the landlord, who had developed a modern outlook, advised to call in the civil surgeon from Balasore. But how could that be possible? An Englishman who ate beef and pork would enter the interior of a holy Hindu house wearing leather shoes and take a look at an unmarried girl and prescribe her the diet of wine and meat! It could never be permitted. Most of his friends, orthodox in temperament, disapproved of the proposal and it was dropped: However, the kaviraj of Balasore and the royal physicians of Nilagiri and Baripada were called in.

The royal physician of Nilagiri observed: "The infection of the marrow has caused this fever. It will take a long time to cure."

The one from Baripada studied her pulse for a long time and remarked: "No, it is not an infection of the marrow.

I find that it is caused by some infection in the bones. You have not studied the science of medicine properly. The way you make the diagnosis you can send not only Govinda Chandra Mardaraj but also all other emperors of the world to heaven."

This made the physician from Nilagiri furious.

"What! I am none other than Jambeswara Tripathy, the son of the royal physician Vighneswara Vaidyaraj, the grandson of Maheswara Sarbavouma. Is there anyone in Orissa who does not know me? You challenge my knowledge of medicines!! Just tell me how many critically ill patients have you yourself cured? If it can be proved that this fever is not caused due to infection of the marrow, I shall give up taking pride in being the grandson of Maheswara Sarbavouma," he shot back.

Narasingha Tihadi, who came from Balasore, listened to these arguments and said:

" I don't agree with either of you. It appears that neither of you have read a single alphabet from the books on medicines. In my diagnosis, the symptoms are related to the infection of the skin. If physicians like you are allowed to practice medicine, then it is not unlikely that all the kings in the feudatory states will die a premature death."

The landlord, Jagabandhu Pattnaik, noticed that the situation was going out of hand. He had called in all these famous physicians to treat his only child who was as precious to him as his own life. He had hoped that when a number of doctors came together, they would consult one another and suggest the correct treatment after making a proper diagnosis. He was disappointed to find these physicians contradicting one another. He was afraid that such disputes in the patient's room would harm rather than help her. He therefore said very politely.

"I have called you, at this hour of crisis, hoping that you will examine the patient together and suggest proper treatment, but you don't seem to agree with one another. The way you have started arguing might aggravate her suffering instead of assuaging it. I beg of you with folded hands that all of you should sit together in the terrace outside and decide on a proper treatment judging the symptoms you have noticed.

Chapter XIV

Diagnosis of the Disease

It was past evening; the landlord sat on the terrace, resting his back on a cushion. The half moon shed white beams of light illumining the courtyard that spread below the terrace. The gentle breeze, sweet and cool, like the sprinkling of ambrosia caressed the body. But it could not help cool the pangs of sorrow that smouldered in the landlord's heart. Not far away from the landlord, his cousin Srihari sat on the mattress. The servants, attendants and officials of the landlord assembled on the stone platform in the courtyard. Purushottama Senapati too was present there. Padmamali's pain had reached its peak that day; her condition was critical. The landlord was terribly upset seeing his only daughter in such misery; his face looked grief-stricken. His sorrow cast its reflection, genuine or fake, on the faces of the people gathered there. All were quiet, Srihari broke the silence: "I appreciate Narasingha Tihadi's opinion. You (addressing the landlord) better take his advice and let him decide the treatment."

"These royal physicians are of no use. The medical expertise which Maheswara Sarbavouma's son Vighneswara

Vaidyaraj had exhibited can be acknowledged only by the kings," Purushottama Senapati told.

One of the of officials present in the crowd queried; "Why do you say so?"

"Once when the king was young," Senapati narrated, "the queen fell ill. The royal physician Vighneswara Vadyaraj was called in. He heard all details about the sickness of the queen. But how could he start treatment without studying the patient's pulse? Could a man other than the king ever be allowed to enter the queen's apartment to hold her hand? The doorman brought the problem to the knowledge of His Majesty. His Majesty sent words that a stranger would not be allowed to enter the queen's chamber even if that meant that her illness would go untreated. Then the Vaidyaraj thought of a way. He appeared before the king and said that His Majesty was right in taking such a well-considered decision. I shall not enter the queen's chamber and hold the queen's hand, he assured the king, 'but I, son of Maheswara Sarbavouma, cannot afford to stand aside and watch Her Majesty suffer in this manner. I have thought of an alternative. I shall stand at the servants' entrance; a length of cord will be tied around the queen's wrist and led through the door to me. I shall hold the cord and study her pulse."

Srihari: Well, did the king agree to that?

Senapati: No. The king applied his sharp wit and found a problem in it and said:

'I object to your proposal. In the first place, is the queen a prisoner that her wrist will be tied up with a cord? Secondly, even if we overlook this problem as not being so important considering the urgency of the treatment, there is still another difficulty. As long as the string is loose, you cannot make a proper study of her pulse. And if the cord is pulled hard it will hurt the queen's delicate hand."

The official: Brilliant. Only a king can analyse a situation in this manner.

Srihari: (Not paying heed to him) What happened next?

Senapati: The physician said that the king was right. Even an enemy would not want that the queen should be tied by her wrist. But, for the treatment of a malady a number of compromises have to be reached at. The scriptures also advise that there is no harm in drinking wine if it is taken as medicine. The physician also said that he would make such arrangements that the queen would not be hurt at all.

Another official: How was that possible? Alas! How her delicate hand must have hurt, tied with a cord!"

Senapati: (Vexed) Your small mind cannot understand these matters. But the Vaidyaraj was not a flattering idiot like you."

Srihari: Okay, leave it. What was the king's reply?

Senapati: The king wanted to know what plans the physician had in his mind. The physician told him that keeping in mind that the king might object to his plan he had already thought of an alternative. Had he not thought so, he would never have dared to place such a proposal. He said that a piece of velvet cloth should be tied seven-fold around the queen's wrist and a length of slightly thick silk cord will be tied over the velvet covering; he would then study the pulse holding the cord.

The first official: What marvellous wit!

Senapati: Yes, of course. It would seem marvellous to a fool like you. If your wit and the Vaidyaraj's are compared...."

Srihari: (Interrupts) Let us not discuss that. What did the king say?

Senapati: (Exasperated) Your Head! That's what he said you dimwit!! The king too was no less clever than the great Vaidyaraj!

After a while the Senapati cooled down a bit and continued.

Senapati: He praised the intelligence of the Vaidyaraj profusely and made all arrangements according to his suggestions.

Srihari: What was the result?

Senapati: The consequence of such foolishness was obvious. The king himself told everything to the queen. But the queen was not stupid like the king. When the Vaidyaraj sent the message that he was waiting outside, the queen tied the length of the silk cord around her pet cat's neck and the cord was led through the door to him. The physician examined the cord with his fingertips for a long time; then he held it to his ears. After a prolonged examination he informed the king that the queen was suffering from serious infection of the lungs. He consulted his books and prescribed medicine. But the queen was wiser. I know very well that she did not use that medicine at all. She came around in due course through her own will power. But the king remained under the impression that the Vaidyaraj's medicine had worked.

Srihari: All these royal physicians are frauds. Jagabandhu, I like Narasingha Tihadi's suggestion.

The landlord: Don't ask me; do whatever you think proper.

The discussions were still going on when Laxmana Panda arrived at the scene.

Chapter XV

Laxmana Panda as an Emissary

Laxmana Panda had come as Duryodhana's emissary. But there was no doubts that the timing was wrong, because he found that the person whose marriage he had come to negotiate was seriously sick. He had been in Panchagada for the last fifteen days, but so far he had not found an opportunity to perform the role of a negotiator he had been assigned. Whenever he came to the Patwari's house, he found a number of physicians sitting on the terrace arguing over the patient's symptoms and servants being sent in all directions to collect roots, and barks of medicinal herbs. All the while, the Patwari wore a look of dejection. How could he have broached the subject of Padmamali's marriage in such a situation? Laxmana Panda visited the landlord's house in the morning and evening every day ever since he had arrived at Panchagada. He had to return without speaking out his intentions and having no other engagement, he spent time only in consuming the good food offered by the landlord.

Some well-wishers had advised Patwari to get his horoscope studied to find out if he was under the evil spell of stars. The landlord had called in Rajiv Nahak, the astrologer and had requested him to make a study of his horoscope. According to the calculations of Rajiv Nahak, Saturn was in the seventh house. He had predicted that the evil influence of Saturn would continue to bring him trouble until the Sun entered the asterism of Libra.

Seeing Laxmana Panda in Panchagada, the landlord thought as if Saturn-incarnate had made his appearance. The landlord had exchanged only a few words with Laxmana Panda during those fifteen days. Laxmana Panda had offered his sympathies to the landlord who was passing through such a troubled time. Laxmana Panda had realised that he had landed himself in a deep crisis. How could he broach the topic of marriage of the landlord's daughter in the present circumstances? On the other hand, Duryodhana kept sending reminders. On that very morning he had received a letter from Duryodhana. The gist of the message was that Duryodhana was anxiously waiting for the return of Laxmana Panda and was expecting him every moment. The letter also attributed the delay to the inefficiency of Laxmana Panda.

On receipt of such a letter Laxmana Panda felt annoyed and wanted to accomplish his purpose soon. Along with this letter from Duryodhana, he had also received another one from his own home and learnt that his wife, who, had recently given birth to a baby son and the newborn were seriously ill. He grew worried and made up his mind that, whatever be the outcome, he must speak out his mind today and set out for his village the very next morning.

Now he stepped on to the terrace of Patwari's household with this resolve. At his arrival a hush fell upon everyone; he addressed the Patwari, saying:

"I am leaving tomorrow."

Before the landlord could say anything in reply, Srihari broke in:

"We could not find out the purpose of your visit; however, we feel ourselves very fortunate that you have set your feet in our house. But you have come at such a time that we could not show you proper hospitality, and were not able to treat you in a manner that befits a guest like you."

Laxmana Panda intervened:

"I am satisfied with the hospitality I have received here."

Srihari: You are being sarcastic.

Laxmana: No, I express my genuine feelings.

Srihari: It is a sign of your nobility and modesty; we know that we have failed in extending a befitting welcome you. If we have, taking into account the present trouble we are in, you must excuse us.

Laxmana: There was nothing wanting in the hospitality you have extended to me. I am really very sorry to find you in such a crisis. But everything occurs as per the wishes of the Lord. He will soon relieve you of your sorrow.

Srihari: We feel obliged to you for the sympathy you have shown us. But, as you have said, everything, depends on the will of the Lord.

Laxmana: I learnt in Nilagiri that some mishap took place in Mantri?

This question struck the landlord like the flash of lightning. He thought that this wicked person was Duryodhana's henchman. Perhaps the intention with which he had come was not good.

Srihari said: Yes, there was a mishap. But God came to our rescue.

Laxmana: I am glad to hear this. You must never be telling a lie.

He kept quiet for some time and then said:

"There had been a rumour in the town that when the rain caused confusion in the fair and people ran helter-skelter, Duryodhana, finding Padmamali alone and helpless, brought her with him. In the mean time, some one (the rumour goes that it was the Routray of Mayurbhanja) finding Duryodhana without enough bodyguards attacked him and took away Padmamali by force. That night he kept her in his tent. Evil minded people are exaggerating this matter in different ways."

It seemed as if the sky above had come crashing down on their heads when the landlord and his friends heard this.

Srihari: (Remaining silent for a while) We know the ways of wicked people: they take pleasure in scandalising good people. They always tend to make mountains out of molehills. They don't realise that they stand guilty before God; besides, those who encourage them to spread such scandals are no less guilty.

Laxmana: You are right. But how many people are as prudent as you are? In this world the number of fools is very large. Duryodhana is very upset at the spread of such rumour. He is unhappy that the villain has snatched Padmamali from his hands and had spread such a scandal about her. He has sent me to bring these matters to your knowledge.

Srihari: Duryodhana had played the role of a true friend. He has exhibited the nobilities of his nature. We are very grateful to him.

Laxmana: Duryodhana has sent me here to convey this to you. But since the day I have arrived here, I found you all so upset over the sickness of sister Padmarnali that I could not bring myself to say these things. This morning I received a letter from my home saying that my presence is urgently needed there. I can't delay my departure even by an hour. A week before I came here, my wife had given birth to a son. The letter says that the mother is in a critical condition. I must leave tomorrow morning. But it would not be proper if I leave without letting you know the purpose of my visit. Now I have come here to tell you the reason for which I came to Panchagada, and also to take leave of you. I know that it is not wise to tell you these things in this hour of crisis. But how can I leave without fulfilling the purpose for which I have come? Thinking that it may help you rather than harm, if I do so, I have brought these matters to your knowledge. You must excuse me if I have made a mistake.

The landlord, who had been silent all the while, spoke:

"You have done a great service by giving us all the facts. You can well see the terrible time we are passing through at present. You must try to understand the seriousness of the situation and forgive us if there was anything lacking in our hospitality."

Laxmana: I am absolutely satisfied with the treatment and attention I have received here.

After keeping quiet for some time Laxmana Panda resumed:

"Now I shall take leave of you." He stood up. Others stood up too.

"You have been so very decent that I acknowledge you as one of my dearest friends. I would like to tell you another thing if you don't take it amiss," Panda said.

The people who had gathered there thanked Panda in one voice. Panda continued:

"Padmamali has attained marriageable age; people

will start gossiping if her marriage is delayed any further."

Srihari: You are right.

Laxmana: Have you found a groom yet?

Srihari: Not yet.

Laxmana: Well, I have a suggestion. You may accept the proposal or reject it. Don't you think Duryodhana Das will be a proper match for her?

Srihari: Of course! Where can we find a better candidate than him? If we send the proposal, will he turn it down? However, at present we are not in a position to think of her marriage. We will send a mediator to Duryodhana Das after she recovers from her illness.

After these discussions the meeting came to an end.

Chapter XVI

Jagabandhu Consults his Wife

"The sacred Laws that Sukracharya framed
And the Vedas that Vrihaspathi explained
Advise husbands
To hold in high esteem
The counsel of a wife."

It was past midnight. The landlord, Jagabandhu
Pattnaik, having finished his dinner, stretched himself on
the bed. The mattress he lay upon was soft and covered
with an expensive, brocaded sheet. But the goddess of
sleep does not always visit a man, who reclines on a soft,
milky white bed. Take the case of the palanquin-bearers;
after bringing down the heavy weight of the palanquin
from their shoulders and satisfying their hunger with the
simple meal of rice flakes when they lie down on a bed of
earth, they experience an unalloyed peace. But does the
palanquin rider who gets borne on their shoulders, and
who eats delicious food and sleeps on a luxurious bed, ever
enjoy such bliss? The answer will undoubtedly be a "No".
That is why I say that the goddess of sleep does not always
appear on luxuriously designed, soft, expensive beds.
Moreover, if the person, who lies on the bed, is troubled
with mental worries, it is obvious that the goddess of sleep

is extremely displeased with him. The landlord was now in a similar plight. After dinner he went to bed. But sleep did not come to his eyes easily. He felt restless and kept turning on his sides. "I am a very unfortunate father," he said to himself. "I can't bear to see the suffering of Padmamali any more. Lord Almighty, why did you bless me with such a gem as Padmamali if you had this in your mind? She is everything I have. She is my son and my daughter; I can't see her in such pain." Overcome by grief, Pattnaik buried his face in his pillow.

Padmamali's mother, Chitralekha finished her domestic chores; she remained present to make sure the servants ate well, but she did not drink even a drop of water herself. When she was through with these duties, she entered her daughter's room. The girl that lay quietly on the bed bore no resemblance to the Padmamali we had seen earlier. Her face had lost its freshness. It looked like a bud of lotus that has withered away even before its petals had opened up. She was pale and emaciated. Tears trickled down the blue, lotus-like eyes of Chitralekha as she saw the miserable condition of her beloved daughter. Padmafnali was in a deep sleep. The physicians, having consulted one another, had administered some sedative to her. Chitralekha warned the maid attending Padmamali to keep a careful watch during the night and came out of the room. She entered her own bedroom; her eyes were still wet with tears. The sight of her tear-filled eyes added to the sorrow of the landlord. He felt utterly miserable.

Husband and wife kept looking at each other's face for some time; both were speechless. Jagabandhu raised himself and sat up. He asked Chitralekha to sit beside him. After she sat down, the landlord asked: "How is Padmamali?"

"She was asleep when I came here."

"So many physicians have come but no one is able to make the correct diagnosis. What else is this if not our bad luck?"

Chitralekha remained silent. The landlord continued: "You are keeping quiet. I am now at my wit's end. I feel hopeless unless I consult you in any every matter. You are my Vrihaspathi, the divine counsellor. Do you know that another misfortune has befallen us?"

"What is it? I feel scared."

"That wicked Duryodhana is the root cause of our trouble. He has sent a meditator. I don't know what devil had taken possession of me that I sent my child to Mantri."

"Mediator? What mediator? Why would Duryodhana send him?"

"He wants to marry Padmamali."

"What do you say! The villain has gone that far?"

"What is to be done now?"

"Ask the mediator to tell you how Duryodhana dared to send such a proposal."

"It would, be, better to leave Padmamali in a forest amidst the ferocious animals than to give her in marriage to someone like Duryodhana. But the fellow is wicked and can create trouble for us. I can rest peacefully if I could give her in marriage soon to a suitable groom. But where shall I get such a person? When she is lying sick and in such a state, should I send people in different directions to seek a bridegroom for her instead of taking proper measures to get her cured? What would people say?"

The landlord fell silent after he said this.

Chitralekha : I can't understand the cause of this sickness. Even skilled physicians are not able to determine the exact cause. I suppose that she is oppressed, by some mental worries. Her suffering will not come to an end unless she is relieved of that.

"Why should anything worry her? She is but a child now!"

"No. She is not a child any more. I have noticed a change in her since she returned from Manrri. She is no more jolly and cheerful as she used to be earlier. She does' not want to talk to anyone now. Most of the time she remains silent, as if she is brooding over something."

"What does she think about?"

"My guess is that Padmamali is thinking of the young man whom I had met in the monastery of Mahanta at Deulasahi. He rescued Padmamali from Duryodhana. When I saw him, l had thought that perhaps Providence had arranged circumstances so that we come across the most suitable groom for Padmamali. As far as I could see, both of them were drawn to each other."

"Who was he?"

"I can't say that. But from his looks it was certain that he hails from a noble family."

"A new thought has come to my mind after hearing this. It is heard that the Routray Prithviraj Bhanja had saved Padmamali from Duryodhana. I can't help it if she has taken an interest in him. To get the younger brother of Maharaja Jadunath Bhanja as my son-in-law! It is unthinkable on my part. The suffering of Padmamali, Duryodhana's message and the information you have given me now, all these things have rendered me incapable of thinking clearly."

"The young man I met at Mahanta's place was not the Routray, because I had seen the Routray in Mantri. But his manners and his bearings were like those of a prince."

"Well, he is not the Routray; still, he is a prince. Which prince had come to Mantri? I am unable to arrive at any conclusion."

"He may or may not be a prince; but the Mahanta said

something that makes me guess that there will not be any serious impediment in the marriage between Padmamali and the young man."

"What did the Mahanta say?"

"Before we left, Padmamali went to the Mahanta to pay her respects. The Mahanta took her chin in his hands and looked at her face for a long time. Then he turned his eyes to the young man and said: "These two are definitely made for each other; perhaps they are some heavenly angels, cursed to be born as human beings."

"This news has revived my hopes. Your wit and discretion have helped me out of many critical situations, This is a very serious affair. What do you suggest we should do?"

"In my opinion, it would be better if we visit the monastery and spend a few days there."

"You are right. The change of place may help her to regain her health. There may also be a chance of her meeting the young man. Besides, Duryodhana will not dare to bring any harm to us at Mayurbhanja. Chitralekha, you have found the correct solution. I am not wrong when I say that you are my most wise counsellor. Tomorrow itself I shall send a letter to the Mahanta." Jagabandhu said cheerfully.

He looked fondly at Chitralekha face, beautiful as a portrait sketched by a skilful artist and said:

"Chirralekha, where are your wits stored? Are they kept hidden in these large, blue-lotus like eyes?"

Chitralekha did not say anything in reply to this. Jagabandhu kissed her charming face and felt as if his heart has been relieved of an enormous weight. The couple, feeling greatly relieved after this discussion, went to sleep.

Chapter XVII

King Parikshita Singh Bhujanga Mandhata Virata Basanta Harichandan

I shall today take the readers to a new place, the massive entry-gate of the royal palace of Kaptipada. With naked scimitars in hand, a couple of sentries were keeping guard over the gate. A number of supplicants from different sections of society assembled before the gate expecting financial help from the king. Before the king went to the garden to enjoy the evening breeze he was supposed to meet them. Everyone was waiting eagerly for the king to make his appearance. Someone waited to seek financial help to perform the death anniversary of his deceased father; another waited to ask for royal charity, without which the marriage ceremony of his daughter could not be solemnized. An old Brahmin stood waiting to seek the king's help in order to perform the sacred thread ceremony of his ten-year-old son. Damodar Narendra Ray, the head guard at the fort kept waiting there to make a complaint that some of the soldiers at the fort have turned rebels. There was Krupasindhu Mahapatra, who came to inform that the work of the government could not be carried out since some wicked tenants had refused to supply him with labourers. Ratnakar Bhutia had come with a grievance that Chhanchana Singh had dispossessed him of his oil mill, which was under his ownership for the preceding three generations. Daitari Pawan Singh had received a threat from his neighbour Fakira Pradhan; he had come to beg royal favour in order to avenge the humiliation. Besides these subjects, a platoon of soldiers was present to escort the king to the garden.

Dear readers, enter the main gate. Walking through the ornate portals of the royal palace, you will arrive at the courtroom. Here you will find the dewans, the supervisors, the almanac reader, the king's personal advisors, the storekeeper and the treasurer, surrounded by the staff of their respective departments, busy at work. Beyond the courtroom, there was the vast, lovely expanse of a flower garden. The garden was brilliant with several kinds of spring-blossoms that lent their fragrance to the gently blowing south breeze. At some places, amidst the flowering plants, there were shrubs and creepers laden with flowers too, enhancing the garden's beauty. In the middle of the garden lay a high, octagonal stone-built platform. From an artificial fountain in front of this platform, the spraying-mist of water was borne away by the breeze and mingled with the fragrance of the flowers. The king sat on the platform on an ornately brocaded mattress, propped up on a soft pillow and enjoyed the gentle evening breeze. Harihara Bhramarabara sat on one side, on another seat. They were alone. At the time when the reader made his entry into the garden, the king Parikshita Singh was speaking. ·

The king: No Hari Babu, I cannot accept your proposal. It is my wholehearted wish that Manorama, my sister, should be the queen. But your ambition seems unachievable.

Hari Babu: You are saying this because you are not aware of the present conditions of Nilagiri state. With the help of only five hundred soldiers, I can easily usurp the throne of Nilagiri. According to my spies, the subjects of Nilagiri are so oppressed that they will not offer the slightest resistance to the attack. They rather want that I should take over the throne as soon as possible.

The king: I do not have much faith in your spies. It may be that the subjects of Nilagiri are oppressed because the state is under the rule of a king, who is a minor, and some trouble mongers and mutineers may be instigating them to tum rebels. Even then your proposal does not seem feasible as Nilagiri is under British rule. Had the Marathas been in power, you could have seized the state by force.

Hari Babu: My spies are trustworthy. The spies of kings like you may tum disloyal. The districts ruled by the Mongols have come under the British rule. But the British have still not been able to control the affairs of the Gadajat states.

The king: Whatever you may say, I cannot bring myself to rely upon your spies. You say that the British have not yet been able to establish their control over the Gadajat states. If this is so, how have they prohibited our practice of collecting the ferry tax? How have they made Trivikrama Bhanja ascend the throne of Mayurbhanja after the death of queen Sumitra Devi?

Haribabu: The state of affairs in Nilagiri is not the same as that prevails in Mayurbhanja. The subjects of Nilagiri do not want prince Krishna Chandra to be the king, because his mother hails from a Mohanty family.

Parikshita Singh remembered Padmamali when the Mohanty family was mentioned.

"Nevertheless, the British have chosen him the king, ignoring your blood ties with the royal dynasty," he said. "They have made you only a pensioner. Under these circumstances, if you create any trouble there the British will certainly punish you. It is my advice that you must desist from making such attempts."

Hari Babu remained silent, as he did not find an answer to this. Just then the doorkeeper approached them with folded hands and informed them that Mahanta Harihara Das stood waiting at the entry- gate of the palace.

The king ordered that the Mahanta be immediately ushered in to his presence. Turning to Hari Babu, he said: "You know how fond I am of Manorama. I shall feel proud if your position and prestige are enhanced. But, at present, I don't approve of your plans. You think over the matter seriously. I am sure, if you judge things in a calm and unbiased mind, you will realise that I am not wrong."

Hari Babu assured him that he would do so and took his leave.

Chapter XVIII

The Mahanta Visits Kaptipada

By this time, the readers must have guessed, without any difficulty that Parikshita Singh, the young man, who had come to Padmamali's rescue, was none other than the king of Kaptipada. During his conversation with Hari Babu, he had suddenly remembered Padmamali; the news of the Mahanta's arrival filled every corner of his heart with her memory. He could not understand, why the Mahanta had come without prior notice. The king felt worried.

The Mahanta was ushered into the king's presence. The king paid his respects to him joining his hands together and bowing his head. The Mahanta was offered the seat, which Hari Babu had vacated. After the Mahanta took his seat, they enquired about each other's wellbeing. Then Parikshita Singh asked: "May I please know the reason that has made you pay this unexpected visit?"

The Mahanta: I felt obliged to come here without giving prior notice to Your Majesty.

Parikshita Singh: I assume that some urgent mission has brought-you here. I am ready to extend whatever help I can to you in accomplishing it.

The Mahanta: I was sure that His Majesty would

grant my wish. Were it not so, I would never have presented myself before him.

Parikshita Singh: You treat me as your son. I shall feel gratified if I can be of any help in fulfilling your wish.

The Mahanta: After His Majesty has promised thus, the purpose of my visit can be kept a secret no longer.

Parikshita Singh: Order me. I know that you will never ask me to do something unjust and improper.

The Mahanta: Before I disclose the purpose of my visit, I have a question.

Parikshita Singh: Please don't hesitate to put it to me.

The Mahanta: Well, do you still remember the incident that occurred in the festival of Jagara at Mantri?

Parikshita Singh: I can never forget that.

The Mahanta: Why? His Majesty has earned undying glory by rescuing a helpless girl from the clutches of a villain. Such instances of bravery and chivalry are of course not easily forgettable.

Parikshita Singh: I cannot agree with you on this. I have just performed the duty of a king by saving Padmamali from the evil hands of Duryodhana. I don't deserve any praise for that. I cannot forget that incident for another reason. Someone within me keeps telling me that the happiness of my life depends on Padmamali. It was preordained that I would save her from danger.

The Mahanta: I am unable to understand what you mean by that.

Parikshita Singh : I believe that you love me as your own son. I have no hesitation in laying open my heart before you. Padmamali's beauty and her good nature have enchanted me. There is no happiness for me in this life without her.

Mahanta had not expected that his mission would be

accomplished so easily. When the king frankly expressed his love for Padmamali, the Mahanta felt extremely glad and said: "I now believe that your union with Padmamali is preordained. It is my sincere wish that you and Padmamali be happily united in wedlock. My blessings are with you."

Parikshita Singh: I have a small reservation. Has anyone in our family married a girl from a Mohanty family?

Mahanta: You need not worry about that. Ramachandra Bhujanga and his brother Janardan Bhujanga had migrated from Chot Nagpur to Nilagiri. They were the founders of the kingdoms of Kansari, Kaptipada and Nilagiri. In course of time, Ramachandra Bhujanga became the chief of Kalahandi fort in Sambalpur district. Janardan Bhujanga, who was, the founder of the royal dynasty of Kansari, had two great grandsons, Narayan Singh Bhujanga Mandhata Virat Basanta Harichandan and Arjuna Singh Bhujanga Mandhata Virat Basanta Harichandan. You are the progeny of Arjuna Singh. Narayan Singh had married Karala, the daughter of Pratap Rudra Deb, the Maharaja of Orissa, and settled at a place called Ghodabatai. His son, Uttareswara Das Harichandan, had come to rule Panchagada by the grace of a saint named Nilagiri and changed its name from Panchagada to Nilagiri. The last king of the state of Nilagiri, Govinda Chandra Mardaraj Harichandan had married Chitra Devi, the daughter of Madhusudan Pattnaik. Doesn't she come from a Mohanty family? She is the mother of Krishna Chandra Deb, the minor king of Nilagiri. Hence, marrying a girl from a Mohanty caste had not been unprecedented in your family.

Parikshita Singh: I feel so relieved!

The Mahanta asked: Have you received any news of Padmamali in the meantime?

Parikshita Singh: No.

The Mahanta: After they returned to their village, the wicked Duryodhana had sent a proposal of marriage through a mediator.

Parikshita Singh's blood boiled when he heard this. "How dare that shameless scoundrel do so"? he said angrily. "What was the landlord's reply?"

The Mahanta: Padmamali was seriously ill when the mediator arrived. The landlord told him that he could not decide anything under the circumstances. He said that he would think over the matter and send his reply. However, expecting trouble from the villain, he is now staying at the monastery with his family. Padmamali's sickness, though not cured, has not got worse since she has arrived at the monastery. It will be great if you can manage to pay a visit to the monastery one of these days.

Parikshita Singh: 'You need not have to say any more. I will go there very soon.

Satisfied that he had accomplished his mission, the Mahanta took leave of the king.

Chapter XIX

The Engagement

Jagabandhu Pattnaik, taking his wife and daughter with him, arrived at the monastery. The Mahanta gladly welcomed them. When he saw Padmamali, emaciated from illness, he understood that the agony of separation from her lover was the root cause of her malady. He had no doubt that if she stayed a few days at this monastery and got an opportunity to meet Parikshita Singh, she would get back to her earlier self. That was why he had gone to meet the king in the royal palace of Kaptipada. He had made adequate arrangements in the monastery for proper treatment of these guests. Padmamali was extremely happy to be able to enjoy the company of Jayanti. After a long time, she had found a friend before whom she could unburden her heart. When Jayanti found Padmamali in such a condition she could not hold back her tears.

Padmamali: An unknown fear oppressed my heart since the time I went home leaving you all. Try as I might, I failed to overcome it. We decided to come here again, and I hope only here the fear could be overcome.

Jayanti: You have no reason to feel scared, because the person to whom you have lost your heart has made it clear that there would be no happiness in his life without you. He has presented you the token of his love. You are not unfortunate like me, who has no hope left.

Padmamali: Still, I feel very anxious when I think of the vast gulf that separates us and, moreover, I do not know who he is. Duryodhana comes to my mind often and I realise that he is the most formidable obstacle threatening our union.

Jayanti: The king of Kaptipada has arrived here today. You will soon become his queen. Why do you make yourself suffer, worrying unnecessarily? Come, let us pluck these beautiful jasmine flowers and make a garland, I shall deck you both with it and watch the lovely sight.

Padmamali and Jayanti gathered a lot of flowers from the garden and strung a beautiful garland. They were merrily talking to each other when Parikshita Singh appeared on the scene. Jayanti saw him and said: "How cruel you are! See what you have done to my dear friend."

When Parikshita Singh saw Padmamali, pale and gaunt, he said: "Her condition was so serious! Why I was not informed?"

Jayanti: You kept your identity a secret from us. How could we have informed you?

Parikshita Singh: It would have been enough if word had been sent to the Mahanta.

Jayanti: All this was destined to come to pass. We shall be glad to see you both united in wedlock soon.

Parikshita Singh: How can the wedding take place before the completion of one year after the death of my father?

Jayanti: The wedding proper, complete with all the rituals, may wait. But where is the harm if you get married exchanging flower garlands?

She told this and signalled to Padmamali. Padmamali adorned Parikshita Singh with sandal wood paste and flower garlands. Parikshita Singh too decorated her hair, her neck and her wrists with flowers and said: "See, how beautiful she looks!"

Jayanti made Padmamali sit beside Parikshita Singh and said:

"To which divine pair should I compare this couple? Radha and Krishna? Rama and Sita? Shiva and Durga or Rati and Kandarpa?"

Saying so, she discretely left the place. We too shall bring down the curtain over this scene.

Parikshita Singh had to return to Mayurbhanja soon afterwards and he could not stay for more than a week in the monastery. But before his departure, a formal engagement ceremony was performed with great pomp. The wedding was to take place in the month of Margashira.

While she bade farewell to Parikshita Singh, Padmamali said: "When I am with you, I feel as if I hold the heaven in my hands, but in your absence, the world is reduced to a meaningless void."

Parikshita Singh: We have spent so many days away from each other. Few more will pass quickly and then all hindrances in the way of our union will disappear.

Padmamali: But my heart is full of misgivings. It seems as if someone keeps warning me that the future will not be safe. Who will guarantee that wicked Duryodhana will not create any mischief when he comes to know of our engagement?

Parikshita Singh: Does he amount to anything? Yet, if the villain attempts to make mischief, I shall wreak havoc on the state of Nilagiri.

After this the lovers bade farewell to each other.

Chapter XX

Duryodhana's Conspiracy

It was afternoon; Duryodhana sat in his garden and leisurely smoked opium, savoring the smell. An old woman sat on the ground near him. I do not really wish to bring the readers into a close contact with this depraved old woman. Yet, I can't but introduce her briefly here.

She was not born a prostitute. She was a housewife, who lived with her family once upon a time. But she became a widow a few days after her marriage. Finding the life of a widow unbearable, she left the house of her in-laws with the help of a neighbour. The person in whom she had reposed her confidence did not have the means to support her. Soon she found herself alone and without a shelter. She started to cash in on her youth, satisfying lecherous men with her body. Eventually the treasure of her youth got exhausted. Helpless, she had to seek the support of those who were once intoxicated with her youth. Duryodhana was one among those who had lent her support. The old woman had spoilt the lives of a number of girls belonging to respectable families, to satisfy his lust. She earned her livelihood by keeping Duryodhana in good humour.

On his return from Mantri, Duryodhana had related the episode of Padmamali to this old woman. She had arrived here today with a shocking news.

Old Woman: Haven't you heard the news?

Duryodhana: What news?

Old Woman: The lion's prey has been snatched away by a jackal.

Duryodhana: What do you mean?

Old Woman: You sit here without a bother, and Padmamali is going to marry someone else.

Duryodhana: Really? Such impertinence? The landlord will give his daughter in marriage to another person ignoring me? He had fooled Laxmana Panda taking advantage of his stupidity. Do you know whom she is going to marry?

Old Woman: I don't know exactly, but I have heard that the groom belongs to a very rich family in the state of Mayurbhanja.

Duryodhana exploded when he heard this.

"Well," he shouted, "let us see how the landlord who is but a subject of this kingdom, would marry his daughter to someone in another kingdom?

The old woman: You must not get angry. Anger always prevents people from reasoning clearly. Is Padmamali so beautiful? Have you ever seen the daughter of the Gadanayak of Ghantashila? What is the beauty of Padmamali compared to hers?

Duryodhana: There is not another beautiful woman in the three worlds who is fit to be the maid of Padmamali.

Old woman: The daughter of the Gadanayak of Ghantashila is not bad to look at. Her marriage is fixed with Dalabehera of Srirampur.

Duryodhana: All right, I shall then snatch both these

girls by force. I shall see who is going to stand in my way. You go. I must meet the queen at once. I swear that I shall keep these two girls with me and make them my slaves. If I can't do this, my name is not Duryodhana.

Chapter XXI

People of one's own sect are the most envious

It was five o' clock in the evening. In the inner section of the palace, Chitra Devi, the queen of Nilagiri reclined on a humble bed spread out on a stone platform. She was not asleep but was resting; propped up on a pillow, her hair sprawled over it. It was a part of the queen's routine to listen to the recital of the Mahabharat in the afternoon. Two maids, Madhavi and Malati, massaged her feet while Kokila recited from the Mahabharat in a voice more melodious than that of the cuckoo. She was reading the Sabha Parva, which dealt with the game of dice between the Pandavas and the Kauravas in the palace of Hastinapur.

The pious and honest Yudhistira lost all his material possessions to shrewd Shakuni and expressed his desire to bring the game to an end. Shakuni, acting upon the instruction of wicked Duryodhana, would not let him off so easily. He said:

"You still possess queen Draupadi. You can stake her. If you win, you will get all your property back, but mind you, in case you lose, you shall have no right over her."

The sarcastic words of Shakuni stung Yudhistira, now

deprived of everything he had, like the fangs of a poisonous serpent. He had a lawful claim over Draupadi. Shakuni had challenged him to stake that claim in the game, he thought sadly to himself. But he was a Kshyatriya after all, and it had always been a sacred duty of a Kshyatriya to accept challenges of all kinds. Yudhistira probably was in the grip of the evil star, Saturn; he agreed to accept the challenge.

The courtiers of Hasthinapur hurled a thousand abuses at Shakuni in their hearts. The gallant Pandava brothers, including Arjuna, hung their heads in shame. The sinewy Bhima glared at him and clenched his jaws in impotent rage. But he could not bring himself to defy Yudhistira who, being his elder brother was as revered as his father. The dices were thrown.

Fate perhaps had turned hostile to Yudhistira. He lost Draupadi. In order to complete the humiliation of the vanquished Pandavas, Duryodhana ordered Draupadi to be brought to the court and Dushasana dragged her to the court pulling her hair. Not satisfied even with this, Duryodhana asked Dushasana to disrobe Draupadi. Shock and shame left the courtiers dumbfounded. Dushasana began to pull at her saree. In utter agony Draupadi started praying to Lord Krishna, the saviour of the distressed. Dushasana kept on pulling at her saree, heaping them down on the floor, but could not strip her as the length of her saree kept on growing endlessly. Dushasana collapsed on the floor, exhausted and the evil purpose of Duryodhana got defeated. The courtiers joyfully hailed the victory of Dharma, the Justice.

Kokila had recited up to this point, when another maid came in and announced the arrival of Duryodhana Das. The Queen was startled at the mention of the name 'Duryodhana'. She raised herself off the bed and walked down to the, servants' entrance where Duryodhana stood waiting. Since Duryodhana was reared up in the house of Madhusudan Pattnaik, there were no restrictions in his speaking to the queen personally,

"Let Her Majesty look after her kingdom; I can't manage it anymore," Duryodhana said.

Queen: Why? What is the matter?

Duryodhana: How can I manage the affairs of the state when the subjects insult me?

Queen: Who has insulted you? How could he dare do so?

Duryodhana: Yes, Your Majesty, I am telling the truth: I'm ashamed to show my face to anyone. I hang my head in shame.

Queen: Why don't you come to the point?

Duryodhana: Your Majesty, forty rupees out of the last year's annual revenue was due on him. This, year, he has not paid the half yearly tax. My fault was that I had demanded that the arrears of last year and the half yearly tax of the current year be paid together. He refused to pay the tax under the pretext that his daughter's marriage is drawing near. I can't bear to utter the words of abuse, he hurled at Your Majesty. He even called Your Majesty the daughter of a lowly Mohanty family and so on. The things he said can't bear a repetition here.

The Queen: Who could have such impudence?

Duryodhana: Who else but the landlord of Panchagada, Jaggu Patwari?

The Queen: Has Jaggu Patwari become so insolent?

Duryodhana: He looks down on people, because he has had a respectable ancestry. People say that the king of Kaptipada is going to be his son-in-law.

The Queen: Well, get him arrested tomorrow. Hold

him in the prison until he pays his tax dues. Put all his property to auction and recover the arrears from him.

Duryodhana: It is my duty to obey the commands of Her Majesty. I had sent messengers for the collection of Her Majesty's revenue, but I was insulted. Now that I am ordered to arrest him, I shall present him before Your Majesty tomorrow. There is one more matter to be placed with Your Majesty's permission.

The Queen: Speak.

Duryodhana: The soldiers of Ghantashila have become mutinous and decided to join hands with Hari Babu.

The Queen: Send a troop of fifty soldiers and get the Gadanayak of Ghantashila arrested.

Chapter XXII

Padmamali Abducted Again

Having received the orders from the Queen, Duryodhana returned home feeling elated. He thought; "Now, let us see if the Patwari fears Duryodhana Das or not." Next day, the soldiers got the Patwari arrested. He was brought before Duryodhana. Jaggu Patwari said that he had no arrears due on him. As regards the half yearly tax, he said, he could not pay it in time because he was to meet the expenses of the marriage ceremony of his daughter, which was drawing near. However, he assured to clear all his dues at the time of payment of annual revenue. Duryodhana could have shown leniency. In fact, some other landlords were also defaulters. Some of them had not even paid their dues for the past two or three years. But Jaggu Patwari' s offence was unpardonable. He had rejected a powerful man like Duryodhana's proposal to marry his daughter and had fixed her marriage elsewhere. Duryodhana could never forgive that. He was empowered by the order of Her Majesty to imprison Jaggu Patwari. He sent the Patwari to prison without delay. Then he ordered his henchmen, Laxmana Panda, Santi Das and Bhagirathi Pattnaik to proceed to Panchagada with a platoon of two hundred soldiers, raid the village and bring Padmamali by force to Nilagiri.

It was Wednesday the 15th July, in the year 1835. Santi Das and others leading a platoon of two hundred soldiers reached Panchagada. The most important person of the village, Jaggu Patwari was in the prison. His farm hands and other labourers were in the fields busy in weeding, loosening and sifting the soil. The few men present in the village fled in fear. Laxmana Panda and Santi Das entered the landlord's house first. The servants, knowing that it was useless to resist them, asked the female folk to conceal themselves in secret corners of the house. Padmamali, after taking her lunch, had gone to visit Purushottama Senapati's house. Her mother had just sat down at her meals. As she was about to lift the first morsel of food to her mouth, a servant approached and said: "Mistress, the soldiers of Nilagiri have broken into the house. There is no escape, you must hide yourself in a secret place."

Chitralekha put the morsel back on the plate. There was no time to wash her hands. She went into a secret chamber. But before doing so she asked her servants to protect her daughter from the intruders. The soldiers marched into the house; broke the locks of the boxes and took everything they could lay their hands on. They could not find anyone in the house and decided to look in the neighbouring houses. So, they searched every house of the village asking for Padmamali and misbehaved with the female folk. At last, they arrived at the house of Purushotrama Senapati. Since Senapati was the royal blacksmith of the Nilagiri state, they did not harass him. Santi Das ordered him to hand over Padmamali to them. He noticed that Senapati was reluctant to obey the order and said: "Look Senapati, both of us are employed in the same kingdom. We are creating this commotion because of Padmamali. We have molested the wives of many; you will have to face similar treatment if you delay in handing over Padmamali to us."

"You must reap the consequence of this. God will safeguard Padmamali. She is in my house. You may take her; but God will come to her rescue." Senapati warned.

There is nothing much to be said. The villains took Padmamali to Nilagiri in a carriage.

Chapter XXIII

Balabantaray Repents

Being faithful to history is difficult. While relating historical events, a writer has no option but to perform that task in all honesty. I have only done that. The events narrated in the previous chapters indicate that, for the accomplishment of the evil intention of one wicked man several innocent persons were subjected to torture and suffering. The sensitive reader while going through the previous chapters must have felt terribly upset; the chords of his heart must have throbbed with the strains of sympathy and sorrow. I request them to forgive me. I have already said that a writer has no authority to distort historical truth; een a marginal alteration is not permitted. If by relating the sorrowful incidents I have been instrumental in bringing the readers unhappiness and causing them to become angry I offer my humble apologies and seek their permission to prceed with my story.

Jaggu Patwari was in prison. The tenants under his care were in great distress. His daughter, who was dearer to him than his life, was captured by Duryodhana. No one in the village was in a position to find a way out of this crisis. Purushotrama Senapati was a mere blacksmith. Of what help could he be in such a dangerous situation? But omniscient God sometimes helps ordinary persons to solve the most complicated problems.

Looking back at the history of Misagyathas and Evander, one can understand how a mere quadruped could accomplish a difficult task when men of great wisdom had failed to do so. Senapati found himself at his wit's end. While he sat in a vacant mood, Balabantaray appeared before him. After he stood near him for some time Senapati's eyes fell on him and he asked:

"Balabantaray? What brings you here?"

Balabantaray: God only knows the trauma I am passing through since I have returned from Mantri. My heart will not rest at peace unless I do something to help Padmamali to atone for what I had got her into on that day. I am now keeping an eye on all Duryodhana's plans. I came here today to find out what would happen and I have seen everything."·

Senapati: (Absentmindedly) Yes.

Balabantaray: This mishap would not have occurred had I not helped that wicked Duryodhana on that night of Jagara festival. Since that very day, I hold myself guiltier than Duryodhana. I am the root cause of the disaster that has befallen Padmamali. How can I save her from this danger? I have been responsible for bringing Padmamali to the notice of Duryodhana. My sin can only be expiated if I release her from Duryodhana's captivity. But how do I do it?"

Senapati: There is an easy way out.

Balabantaray: Tell me.

Senapati: Through your long association with him, you have earned Duryodhana's trust; you know all his secrets. They have taken Padmamali away. You can find out where she has been hidden. You must make sure that until we release her, the villain does not harm her in any manner. I shall make such arrangements that we can free her very soon.

Balabantaray: I know the place where Duryodhana will hide Padmamali. I will, as advised by you, see to it that Duryodhana is not able to cause any harm to her at least for a week.

Senapati: All right. You go now. I am taking measures for releasing Padmamali within a week.

Balabantaray assured Senapati that he should have faith in him and left the place. Senapati was Patwari's neighbour and his childhood friend. He knew that Padmamali was engaged to Parikshita Singh. He was also aware that the Mahanta had acted as the mediator for this marriage. He, without delay, set out to meet the Mahanta, riding a horse that belonged to Patwari. Before leaving he advised one of Pattnaik's servants to lodge a complaint about the incident at the police station in Balasore.

Chapter XXIV

Senapati in the Monastery

Senapati rode through the forest. The path he took was narrow, lined on both side by thorny shrubs and bushes. The path was difficult to negotiate, but Senapati pressed ahead. He did not bother that the horse's hooves might skid and both the animal and the rider would come to harm. The horse trotted on. He had started at about 4 o' clock in the afternoon. He had covered about ten miles, yet another six miles of the journey lay ahead of him.

As evening approached, a mantle of black slowly descended on the earth and wrapped it up. It seemed impossible to cover the remaining distance in one hour. Senapati, confident that there would be no trouble, did not bring the horse-keeper with him and had preferred to come alone. He was determined to reach the monastery of Deulasahi at any cost. He had no time to think about the condition of the horse. He knew that Patwari was very fond of this horse, but the situation was such that there was no alternative for him but to ride on. That the horse might not survive the stress of the journey, and that he himself might fall and break his neck and his dead body might not be cremated -- bothered Senapati in the least for he had no time to think about such matters. Till now the horse had been trotting along. But such trotting wouldn't be enough. The horse must be made to move faster. He kicked at its flank and whipped it. Spurred by this, the animal leaped ahead like a flame of fire and galloped away with the speed of lightning. Moving with great speed it covered the rest of the distance, in the gathering darkness, in one hour and reached the monastery in Deulasahi. But as soon as Senapati dismounted, the poor animal collapsed on the ground and breathed its last.

Seated on a deerskin, the Mahanta was offering his evening prayers when Senapati arrived. Senapati washed his hands and legs and felt refreshed after the arduous journey. His prayers over, the Mahanta found Senapati waiting. He anxiously asked a series of questions:

"Senapati, what, brings you here? Is everything all right? How is the landlord? When did you start from Panchagada?"

Before the Mahanta could ask any further question, Senapati gave him a detailed account of all that had happened. The Mahanta listened to him, and remained speechless for a while. After a few moments, he said:

"This is the height of depravity. How could the villain be so bold, when there is a British province in the vicinity? Has he no fear of that?

Senapati: Could he dare do this had he been afraid of anything?

Mahanta: What can be done now? Has a complaint been lodged with the magistrate of Balasore?

Senapati: Before coming here, I had entrusted Fakira Parida with that task. But what purposes will that serve? By the time the magistrate comes to investigate, it would be too late. Padmamali is now in the clutches of wicked Duryodhana. Who can guarantee that the villain, finding her alone, would not harm her?

The Mahanta: You are right. What can we do to prevent it?

Senapati: I have come to seek your advice, because I myself could not find a way out.

The Mahanta thought for a while. Then, as if an idea had struck his mind, he blurted out excitedly, Yes! That's it!

Senapati was eager to know what had crossed the Mahanta's mind.

The Mahanta: I have found out a way. Let us send a message to Parikshita Singh. He will set everything right.

The Mahanta immediately made arrangements for sending a messenger to Kaptipada. Senapati spent the night in the monastery and started his return journey at daybreak.

Chapter XXV

The Fire-Ball

Despite Parikshita Singh's refusal to lend him help, Hari Babu had not completely given up the hope of capturing the throne of Nilagiri. The chiefs of a number of villages had come over to his side. Bhagawan Babu and Nanda Babu of Kansari had persuaded Kanhai Babu, the chief of Kansari village to support them. The chiefs of Bhumijas and Kurmis, tribals in Berhampur in the Nilagiri state, had also supported their cause. Patra Parida and Chaitanya Choudhury had joined the band of rebels. The rebels had received assurance from Routray Prithvinath Bhanja that he would help them with a troop of two hundred soldiers. Haribabu was preparing to launch a full-fledged attack on Nilagiri uniting all these groups of soldiers. But, in the meanwhile, he sent small troops of fifty odd soldiers to raid individual villages of Nilagiri and to drive the livestock of the villagers to the rebel camps. ·

As the rebels were preparing for the seize of Nilagiri, the messenger of Mahanta presented himself before Parikshita Singh.

The king listened to everything about the incident

that had occurred in Panchagada. He now rode to the camp of the rebels. He met Hari Babu arid said:

"Hari Babu, I shall lend you three hundred soldiers. Get all soldiers you have been promised by Routray Babu and Kanhai Babu, assembled; we shall march to Nilagiri at the earliest. I along with Bali Babu shall lead the troops of Kaptipada."

Hari Babu, and others were delighted on learning that Parikshita Singh had also joined them and immediately ordered to get the soldiers to assemble. Parikshita Singh instructed his army chiefs to send a 'fire-ball' through a messenger to soldiers of his own state.

We must explain to the readers what a 'fire-ball' was. It was a form of signal to alert the soldiers living in the highlands to get ready for a battle. A burning charcoal would be tied to the upper-end of a Siyari creeper and a messenger carried it to highland villages, where the soldiers lived. Once he gave a fire-ball to soldier, the responsibility of alerting the soldiers in the next village would be transferred to the latter. This way, the fire-ball would change hands and the message would be circulated. This method of alerting the soldiers through a fire-brand was in practice in Scotland. Battles were regular events during those days and sending a fire-ball was the most successful means of alerting the soldiers living in the hills. It was not within the power of anyone to disobey the fire-ball. It was understood that if anyone dared disobey it, his house would be set on fire and he would be punished appropriately.

On that particular day an auspicious event was taking place in the village of Srirampur. It was the marriage ceremony of Govinda Sardar, the Dalabehera; the bride was Jayanti, the daughter of the Gadanayak. The bridegroom was about to board the palanquin. The band of musicians, the torchbearers, the priest and the companions of the groom all were ready to start the procession to the bride's village. The air reverberated with the auspicious sound of the blowing of conches. But what a disaster!! The messenger carrying the fire-ball came up to the bridegroom. While handing over the fire-ball to the groom he uttered a code word "Vendia Tangara". The crowd was struck dumb. Govinda, Sardar Singh, without wasting a moment, shed his bridegroom's costume and proceeded to the next village carrying the fire-ball, The code word meant that the soldiers must assemble, properly armed, at a place called Vendia Tangara.

The next day, before sunset, three hundred soldiers gathered at the above-mentioned place. A platoon of two hundred soldiers sent by the Routray, Prithvinath Bhanja and the rest three hundred mobilised by Hari Babu, eight hundred soldiers in total, camped at Kaptipada, ready to launch an attack on Nilagiri. They elected Parikshita Singh as the commander of the entire army and instructed the soldiers to act upon his commands. On that very night the rebels held a meeting and worked out the strategy of the war. Parikshita Singh said:

"Patra Parida and Chaitanya Choudhury of Berhampur have joined us. Tomorrow, early in the morning, we shall move to Berhampur with our troop and camp there. Nilagiri is not more than five kosha (ten miles) from there. Half the number of our soldiers will remain in Berhampur. The other half will march in the direction of Nilagiri after the evening. They can reach the fort by midnight. There are only five hundred soldiers in the royal army of Nilagiri. Most of them have become rebels. We shall seize the fort during the night. Half the number of our soldiers will be enough for the mission."

The rebels thanked him and agreed with him unanimously.

Let us leave the rebels to do their planning at Kaptipada. Readers, let us come back to Nilagiri and watch what turn the events are taking there.

Chapter XXVI

The March to Ghantashila

The Gadanayak and others eagerly looked forward to the groom's arrival after completing the preliminary rituals of marriage of his daughter Jayanti. The marriage ceremony would be completed after the groom arrived.

It was past midnight. But the groom had not arrived. Nor was there any news from their side. The Gadanayak decided to send someone to find out the reasons for the delay.

In those days, there were some people belonging to the Pana caste, who were experts at walking on stilts. We know that they could effortlessly cover long distances walking on stilts and commit thefts in villages miles away and return home before dawn.

They were known as 'Leaping Tigers'. . ,

The Gadanayak decided to send one such leaping tiger to the groom's village. As soon as the leaping tiger received orders, he walked to the destination and came back just before morning with the news that the groom had already left the village carrying the fire-ball. The Gadanayak felt dismayed at the news and, with a heavy heart, he requested his guests and relatives to leave.

We have learnt in the previous chapter that Duryodhana, acting upon the orders of the Queen, had proceeded to Ghantashila with fifty men after sending a platoon of one hundred soldiers led by Santi Das and Laxmana Panda to Panchagada.

Each village had a Bhagavata house, where holy scriptures were recited in the evening, and a raised platform near it. This was also used as guesthouse for accommodating important guests visiting the village. Riding an elephant Duryodhana arrived at the platform at Ghantashila with his entourage. One of the leaping tigers soon informed the Gadanayak about his arrival.

The Gadanayak smelled trouble. Duryodhana's sudden arrival was not a good sign, he thought. Nevertheless, when a guest had come to the village, necessary hospitality must be shown.The Gadanayak therefore sent a basketful of eatables such as rice, vegetables, pulses, milk, ghee, curd and a variety of sweetmeats etc. He accompanied the basket bearer and paid his respect to Duryodhana. He stood with folded hands. Duryodhana glanced at the basket greedily and said aloud:

"What are these? What should I do with them?"

The Gadanayak said, "Your Majesty has set foot in our village; what could we offer you? I present this humble gift in your honour." He motioned to the bearers of the baskets to move towards the kitchen. Duryodhana felt happy within. Perhaps the readers have not forgotten the real intention with which Duryodhana had come to Ghantashila. But he did not speak anything about the same at that time. He sent back the Gadanayak asking him.to come in the afternoon, after he had his lunch and rested himself.

Duryodhana filled his stomach with the various dishes prepared from the provision sent by the Gadanayak;

then he stretched himself on the soft bed to relieve himself of the fatigue of the journey.

In the afternoon, the subjects of village Ghantashila and of the neighbouring villages gathered in the mango orchard adjacent to the platform. Some came to bring their grievances to Duryodhana's notice; others came out of sheer curiosity. Duryodhana awoke from the midday nap, had a wash and summoned his trusted clerk, Bhajahari Das.

Bhajahari arrived and said:

"My Lord, do you know? Something very interesting happened yesterday."

Duryodhana: What happened?

Bhajahari: The daughter of the Gadanayak of Ghantashila was to be married to Govinda Singh, Dalabehera of Srirampur yesterday. Everyone eagerly awaited the groom's arrival; but the groom did not come. When it was past midnight, the Gadanayak was worried and sent a messenger to the groom's place. The messenger came back with the news that the groom, had left the village with the fire-ball.

Duryodhana: (Anxiously) The Fire-ball? This is not good news. Srirampur is a village of soldiers, which comes under Kaptipada. Could it be that Parikshita Singh has joined hands with Hari Babu?

Bhajahari: Whatever it might be, those people were thoroughly embarrassed. The wedding could not be solemnized.

Duryodhana: That of course is a good news in a way, because we have come here to take that girl.

Bhajahari: People say that she is very beautiful.

Duryodhana: Then that old hag Ramia Maa was right?

Bhajahari : The girl was unwilling to marry Govinda Singh.

Duryodhana : Why?

Bhajahari: The Gadanayak of Ghantashila and the Dalabehera of Srirampur were childhood friends. They had sworn that they would tighten the bond of their friendship by getting one's son married to the daughter of the other. In course of time, the Dalabehera became the father of a son and a daughter was born to the Gadanayak. Their joy knew no bounds. But providence had ordained otherwise. The Gadanayak's daughter fell in love with another young man.

Duryodhana: This sounds like the tale of Savitri and Satyaban. But how are we going to achieve the goal we have set for ourselves?

Bhajahari : Is that such a big problem for Your Lordship?

Duryodhana : I have a plan. Tell me how do you like it.

Bhajahari : Your wish is my command.

Duryodhana: I shall charge the Gadanayak with the offence of conspiring with Hari Babu, arrest him and take him to the fort of Nilagiri. You shall stay back here with the soldiers. At the dead of night, raid the Gadanayak' s house, abduct the girl and bring her to Nilagiri by morning. Get a palanquin and bearers ready.

Bhajahari: This is a fool-proof plan.

Duryodhana: Well, you leave now; I shall come a little later.

A large number of people had gathered in the mango orchard. Bhajahari Das sat on a carpet. Files, containing documents of the estate lay open in front of him. As Duryodhana Das arrived there, the subjects stood up and bowed their heads in respect. Duryodhana took his seat. The subjects also sat down. He glanced at the Gadanayak and asked:

Gajendra, I heard an unfortuneate incident happened yesterday?

The Gadanayak: Yes, My Lord. We had made all arrangements for my daughter's marriage with the Dalabehera of Srirampur. But we were informed that he went off carrying the fire-ball.

Duryodhana: Srirampur comes under the ruler of Kaptipada; why are soldiers being mobilised there with the help of fire-ball?

The Gadanayak: How can I answer that question, sir?

Duryodhana: I presume that you are holding back facts. You know a lot. Did the soldiers of Hari Babu approach you?

The Gadanayak: Which Hari Babu?

Duryodhana : As if you do not know. I am speaking of Harihara Bhramarabara, the brother-in-law of King Parikshita Singh.

Gadanayak : (swallowed) What connection could I have with him?

Duryodhana: No connection? Bhajahari ! Show that letter to him.

Bhajahari took a piece of paper out of his bag and showed it to the Gadanayak and demanded:

"Who is this Lambodara Gajendra, who has written this letter?"

Gadanayak: (Licking his dry lips) I wouldn't know sir."

Duryodhana: Perhaps you will be able to remember everything when you listen to the contents of this letter. Well, Bhajahari, read out the letter.

Bhajahari: (Reads)

I offer my prayers at the feet of Sri Sri Lord Jaggannath. This is a message from Sri Lambodara Gajendra, the

Gadanayak of Ghantashila fort in the name of Sri Patra Parida and Sri Chaitanya Choudhury, the chiefs of the Bhumija and the Kurmi tribes of Berhampur.

Hari Babu's messenger had come here with the information that the Routray of Mayurbhanja, Sri Prithvinath Bhanja and chief of Kansari, Kanhai Babu, had promised to help Hari Babu with their soldiers. Only the king of Kaptipada had not agreed to join him. But Hari Babu is hopeful that events may take such a turn that the king of Kaptipada would be compelled to combine force with the rebels without any hesitation. Hari Babu advised us to keep ourselves prepared for any emergency. We are passing through a period of such anarchy that our womenfolk and our livestock are in grave danger. Even our lives are not safe. Under these circumstances, there is no option but to join hands with Haribabu. Hence, we request you to keep your soldiers in readiness. When Hari Babu arrives, you must accompany him to Berhampur. The testis in the hands of Lord Jagannath. Farewell. The fifteenth day, the month of Mithuna, Sal 1242. Ghantashila, Nilagiri.

Duryodhana: Now, perhaps you understand the purpose behind sending the fire-ball? Don't you?

Gadanayak remained silent:

Duryodhana: It means that Parikshita Singh has agreed to help Haribabu. You, being a subject of Nilagiri, having lived here for generations, now, are conspiring with the rebels.

The Kshyatriya blood that ran in the veins of the Gadanayak, boiled. He could not keep quiet any longer.

"Too much of anything is disastrous," he said heatedly. "The well-being of their subjects should be what should concern the kings most. God will never bless the land where the lives and property of the subjects are not safe. And the rogue who is at the root of such anarchy will be blighted by a divine curse.

Duryodhana: Handcuff this scoundrel and keep him in confinement. The Queen shall herself judge this case of treason. Get the elephants ready. I will leave shortly.

Chapter XXVII

An Unexpected Reunion

Balabantaray was the most trusted and favoured follower of Duryodhana. But his heart ached when he recollected the cruel treatment he had received from him. The rift between the two was apparent. But people thought that this misunderstanding was a temporary thing and would be resolved soon. Balabantaray, having promised to Purushottama Senapati to help Padmamali, appeared at the garden house of Duryodhana one day. He knew that the maidens captured by Duryodhana by trick or by force for satisfying his carnal desire, used to be kept in that garden house in the custody of the old Ramia Maa. There were three rows of rooms in the garden, surrounded by high compound walls. The first row served as the servant's quarters and the kitchen. The two behind it were used to lodge the women Duryodhana brought.

The gardener seeing Balabantaray after a long time welcomed him saying: "What Balabantaray, you have come after a long time?"

Balabantaray: I was not here. I had been to Panchagada. There I heard that Laxmana Panda, Santi Das and others have carried the Patwari's daughter away by force.

Gardener: Yes. She is kept in the rear block. That girl is wailing so bitterly that even the heart of a stone would melt.

Balabantaray: Who is there with her?

Gardener: 'Who else but that old bawd, Ramia's mother.

Balabantahy: Then it is the end for that poor girl!

Gardener: She is not alone. Last night Bhajahari has brought another girl from somewhere.

Balabantaray: Would such sins escape divine justice?

Gardener: Everything depends on God's will.

Balabantaray: The sinners who commit such crime are not the only ones that are guilty. Listen to me, friend, those who watch such sins being committed without protesting are also equally guilty. Where does the old woman stay?

Gardener: She keeps watch over the rooms in the back row throughout the day. She leaves at ten o'clock at night, after dinner.

Balabantaray: It would be a deed of virtue if we rescue the girls from here. It can be possible if you extend a little help. In the meanwhile, let me find out who is the other girl they have brought here.

Saying so, Balabantaray entered the house. He crossed the first row of rooms and came to the next one. It has been mentioned before and it is known to all that Balabantaray was the most trusted follower of Duryodhana, and could go to any place without being checked. He arrived at the main door of the third row of rooms, but found that it was locked from inside. He started inspecting every room in the second row. As he did so, he saw something, which shocked him so much that he could not decide for a while whether he was dreaming or his mind had got disoriented. The person whom he saw was also speechless in astonishment. Both of them were silent for a while. Then Balabantaray called softly:

"Jayanti."

Jayanti: Have the Gods really taken mercy on me and sent you here to rescue me from this boundless ocean of sorrow? Is it true that my year long practice of austerity has finally borne fruit?

In answer, Balabantaray took Jayanti into his lap and kissed her lotus-like lovely face. They experienced a divine ecstasy as their bodies touched each other. Jayanti narrated everything in detail to Balabantaray: how her marriage was fixed with the Dalabehera, how he left carrying the fire-ball, how Duryodhana harassed and humiliated her father, and finally how Bhajahari had brought her here by force.

Balabantaray listened to everything and said:

"No happiness is complete without the experience of sorrow. These are the games that gods play with us humans. Did you ever expect that we would meet again?

Jayanti: Now that I have got you back, my happiness knows no bounds.

Balabantaray: Your joy is boundless! But are you aware of the suffering of someone else?

Jayanti : Who is that?

Balabantaray: "Do you know who is there in the back rooms of this garden -house?"

Jayanti: No. But I always hear the sound of a girl sobbing. That old woman is keeping a constant watch over her.

Balabantaray: Do you know who she is? She is none other than the daughter of the landlord of Panchagada, Jagabandhu Pattnaik.

"Padmamali !!" Jayanti exclaimed.

Balabantaray: (Surprised) Do you know her?

Jayanti then went on to narrate the incidents at Deulasahi, how she had met Padmamali twice in the monastery of the Mahanta. She also told him of the growing intimacy between Parikshita Singh and Padmamali and their engagement. Balabantaray repeated,

"These are only games played by the gods."

Balabantaray looked around the room and discovered a tiny window that was kept closed, He opened it and found that it was fitted with strong wooden bars. He asked Jayanti what lay behind the window. Jayanti said that a backyard, which was common to both the second and third rows of rooms, lay behind it. The gardener had told Balabantaray that the old woman used to leave the place at night. Jayanti confirmed this and told him that the old woman, locked the door of Padmamali's room before leaving. Balabantaray thought for some time, and said:

"Now that God has brought us together in such a miraculous way, He will certainly help me set you free. My frequent visits to this place may arouse the servants' suspicion. I shall come when I find a suitable opportunity. That old woman is very shrewd. We have to be very careful. I shall come tomorrow after dark."

He kissed Jayanti again and took leave of her. Jayanti felt greatly relieved. But she was worried about Padmainali.

Chapter XXVIII

Balabantaray's Atonement

Next day, when darkness of the evening settled over the earth, Balabantaray arrived at Jayanti's room. Both of them enjoyed each other's company till night. When it was time for the old woman to leave, Balabantaray hid himself in an adjacent room. The old woman came out of Padmamali's room and locked the front door. She came to Jayanti and asked:

Daughter, what are you doing?

Jayanti: What can I do, except cursing myself for being born? Why did the Almighty create such an unfortunate woman like me?

Old Woman: Why do you think yourself unfortunate? Don't you think you are lucky that you are going to be Duryodhana Das's darling?

Jayanti: Those who deem it as good fortune, let them do so. But 1 shall escape, this torture only if I die tonight.

Old woman: Why? Do you face any difficulties here? If Duryodhana hears of it, he won't spare my life.

Jayanti: ·This place is so lonely; I don't find even a kitten around here. And you are talking of difficulties!

Old woman: Okay, let me see what I can do about it.

Saying so the old woman left.

Balabantaray came out of his hiding place. He brought a large block of stone and kept it on Jayanti's bedstead so that she could easily reach up to the window. Then he opened the doors of the window and scraped the edges of the wooden bars in such away that they could be removed easily at the time of need and could be replaced again. Both of them climbed down a rope-ladder through the window after removing the wooden bars. They went to the back door of the apartment in which Padmamali was kept confined and to their pleasure and surprise discovered that it was not locked. They entered it and found that the door of Padmamali's room too stood open. In the dim light of the lamp, they saw Padmamali, emaciated and shabbily clad, lying on a bed. As their shadows fell in the room, -Padmamali became aware of human presence and raised her face to find a man and a woman approaching her. Her eyes were bleary through weeping. She could not recognise them properly and an unknown fear cluthched at her heart at the sight of these two. Jayanti called out softly: "Dei" Padmamali recognised the voice and the memory of the past came flooding back to her. She called, "Jayanti !! Is it you?"

Balabantaray lay prostrate on the floor and said:

Sister, please forgive me. I am the root cause of all these troubles. I have sworn that I shall expiate my sin by putting an end to my life if I fail to rescue you from this danger.

Jayanti introduced Balabantaray to Padmamali.

Padmamali: Jayanti is my intimate friend. You are so dear to her. Please get up. What harm have you done to me that you should ask for my forgiveness?

Balabantaray sat up on the floor and said:

I am your slave; please don't embarrass me by treating me as if I am worthy of respect. I don't deserve it. Had I not helped the wicked Duryodhana on that day of the festival of Jagara, this would never have happened. Senapati had already left to consult the Mahanta and find out some way of rescuing you. They would soon take you away from here. But until that happens, it is my responsibility to see that Duryodhana does not harm you.

Padmamali: You are a noble person. You can't be accused of any crime as the accident that occurred during the festival of Jagara. I am glad to learn that Senapati is trying to rescue me. May God help him succeed. I shall remain grateful to you for the help you have rendered me.

Balabantaray: I am a very ordinary person. Please don't address me in such respectful manner. You make me feel ashamed and it gives a lot of pain to me. Whatever I am doing is of no consequence at all. I shall consider myself worthy if I am able to help you even a little. And if occasion arises, I shall look for a reward from Your Majesty.

Padmamali: Okay, I shall not address you in that manner if it hurts you.

Balabantaray thought for a while and then spoke his thoughts aloud:

"Alas! What a cruel fate; the priceless gem, fit to be studded in a royal crown and enhance its worth, will adorn the neck of a swine like Duryodhana! Could even the thought of this be tolerated!!"

Then addressing Padmamali, he said:

Sister, you don't worry, Duryodhana can bring you no harm. I have come to know that Hari Babu, with the support of the troops of the king of Kaptipada, is advancing towards Nilagiri. The king himself is also coming with them. This must have been the work of the Mahanta. We shall have to be alert and careful till they arrive.

Saying so, he took out a sharp blade dagger from under his robe and handed it to Jayanti.

"If necessary, make use of this." He advised her.

Jayanti: (Holding the dagger)

I am the daughter of the Gadanayak of Ghantashila; I can deal with any emergency.

Padmamali slid a ring from her finger and gave it to Balabantaray, who had asked for a token of identity, which would enable him to introduce himself to King Parikshita Singh. Banchhanidhi Balabantaray left the place after paying his respects to Padmamai. Before he left, he carefully replaced the stone, which he had kept on Jayanti's bed.

Chapter XXIX

The Queen Flees

In the morning, word spread in the palace that Hari Babu had camped at Berhampur since the previous night with about one thousand soldiers, intending to invade the fort of Nilagiri and usurp the throne. He would attack the fort any moment. The news alarmed the queen, and she immediately summoned Siva Pattnaik and Duryodhana. She ordered them to ask the soldiers to resist Hari Babu and to make arrangement for herself and her two minor sons to leave for Balasore safely. Thinking that it would be very difficult to organise the soldiers, who would feel demoralised if the queen left the palace at such an hour of crisis, Duryodhana tried to persuade the Queen to give up the idea of going to Balasore. But Duryodhana had to act according to her direction since she would not budge from her decision. Soon she left for Balasore with her two sons.

Duryodhana sent messengers in all directions asking the soldiers to assemble. It was decided that Siva Pattnaik would give battle to the enemy with two hundred soldiers at the mountain- pass at Padmatola and Duryodhana would keep guard over the fort with the rest of the soldiers.

Soldiers in tens and twenties started arriving from

nearby villages. But messengers sent to far off places did not return till midnight. Next day, in the morning, the counting showed that only a few more than three hundred soldiers had assembled. In the afternoon, Siva Pattnaik left with two hundred soldiers. He camped at the peak of the mountain-pass and waited there for the enemy to arrive. Duryodhana posted the rest of the soldiers under his command at different strategic points in and around the fort. He doubled the number of sentries guarding the garden house.

That evening Duryodhana's thoughts returned to Padmamali. She had been in his captivity for some days. He was eager to find out if any change of heart in her had occurred in the meantime. He was frightened at the news of the impending attack by Hari Babu and was doubtful about the outcome of the battle. Hence, he was apprehensive that Padmamali might slip out of his hands. As he pondered over such matters, the old woman appeared before him. On seeing her, Duryodhana asked:

"What is the news?"

"Everything is fine; it will take only a few more days to make her yield to your wish."

"It is not possible to wait any longer. I shall come there tonight." Duryodhana said.

"Please do. However, the two girls are finding their loneliness unbearable as they are kept in separate rooms. If you permit me, I shall put them together. That may have some good result."

"Do so. Has anyone come to meet them?"

"None at all," she assured.

Duryodhana handed a silver coin to the old woman. Delighted, the old woman came back straight to the garden house.

"Look daughter, what a kind-hearted man Duryodhana is," she told Jayanti. "When he came to know that you are feeling lonely, he immediately asked me to get you a companion. Come with me to the other room. There is another girl like you there. Jayanti followed the woman to Padmamali's room. Then the old woman left them there together.

Chapter XXX

Parikshita Singh's Camp

Patra Parida and Chaitanya Choudhury, the leaders of the Bhumija and the Kurumi tribes of Berhampur, joined the rebels at Berhampur with their troops. Together they worked out their future plan of action. It was decided that the troops should be divided into two sections. One section, under the command of Haribabu, would move along the Kansari Street and camp at the mountain- pass at Padmatola; the other, under the leadership of Parikshita Singh, would march down the Kaptipada road and launch an outright attack on the fort of Nilagiri. Accordingly, Parikshita Singh and his battalion, aiming to attack the fort in the darkness of the night, camped in a mango orchard, some three miles away from Nilagiri.

It was past evening. The shadow of night started to drape the earth gently with a mantle of black. The soldiers, in groups, were busy cooking over the camp fires. In front of Parikshita Singh's tent where a fire was blazing, a sentry paced up and down keeping watch. This guard was not a complete stranger to the readers. He was the same unfortunate Dalabehera of Srirampur, who was engaged to marry Jayanti. We know he had to cast off his groom's apparel in order to carry the fire-ball. He had learnt that his would be wife was attracted towards Balabantaray. Govinda had seen Jayanti -- he was sure that Jayanti would have belonged in the category of beautiful women. But, honest and innocent by nature, he was mentally prepared to give her up on learning that she had lost her heart to another man. But the imperceptible ways of Providence had ordained otherwise. As Govinda kept pacing up and down, he noticed a man advancing towards him. When the stranger was within fifty feet from him, Govinda shouted:

"Who is that? Stop there; give me the password or else I shall shoot straight at your chest."

"I am a complete stranger here, I do not know the password," the man replied.

"Why have you come here, then?"

"I want to meet King Parikshita Singh."

"Are you a soldier of Nilagiri?"

"Yes, I am."

"A soldier of Nilagiri! I cannot understand why have you come here?"

"You won't. But your king will. He will not only know me but will also be delighted to see me."

"What is your name?"

"Banchhanidhi Balabantaray."

Govinda was astonished. "You belong to the enemy camp. How can I trust you at this crucial hour, when a battle is at hand?"

"I carry such a token of identity and bring such news that your king will be immensely pleased to see me." Balabantaray spoke with conviction.

"Okay, come here and show me the token."

Coming near, Balabantaray handed him a ring. Govinda noticed that it was the signet ring of king Parikshita

Singh. He called the doorkeeper and sent the ring to the king. The doorkeeper came back almost immediately and asked Balabantaray to follow him. The doorkeeper presented Balabantaray before the king and came out.

Parikshita Singh was reclining on a camp bed. A brass lamp, clamped to the iron chain that hang from the canopy above, shed a bright light illuminating the inside of the tent. Balabantaray paid his respects to the king by lying down prostrate on the floor. He stood up. The king asked:

"Where did you get the ring from?"

Balabantaray: Sister Padmamali gave it to me.

The king: How is she?

Balabantaray: She is alright now. But unless she is released soon, she will be in grave danger. I have learnt that Duryodhana has planned to visit her tonight. That is why I have come to Your Majesty without even a moments delay.

The king: You will be appropriately rewarded for this.

Balabantaray: I don't need any reward Your Majesty. I have taken a vow that I shall kill myself unless sister Padmamali is set free. Your Majesty should not delay.

The king: You must be knowing the place where she is kept confined?

Balabantaray: Yes, Your Majesty. But, I have another piece of news for you. The landlord Jagabandhu Pattnaik and the Gadanayak of Ghantashila have also been taken prisoners.

The King: Why the Gadanayak? What was his offence?

Balabantaray: He has a beautiful daughter. That is his offence. They have kept sister Padmamali and the daughter of the Gadanayak in separate apartments. But by now they might have put them together. Unless we make haste, everything will be lost. Half a mile away from the royal palace of Nilagiri, there is a garden house, which belongs to Duryodhana. They have kept the girls there under lock and key. Duryodhana will visit them around ten o' clock tonight. Siva Pattnaik has already left with a platoon of two hundred soldiers to guard the mountain-pass at Padmatola. There are hardly about a hundred soldiers left in the fort. Your Majesty could easily seize the fort with only two hundred soldiers.

When Parikshita Singh heard this, he summoned Bali Babu and ordered him to immediately march to the fort. He also asked him to appoint Balabantaray as a Sardar and furnish him with the proper uniform and arms.

Chapter XXXI

The Rescue of Padmamali

On receiving Duryodhana's permission, the old woman left Jayanti with Padmamali and went home. United, both the girls experienced immense happiness. The night grew darker. When silence reigned everywhere, Duryodhana, accompanied by the old woman, arrived. Padmamali was extremely frightened at the sight of these people. But Jayanti tried to embolden her and asked her not to fear.

Addressing Padmamali, Duryodhana said:

"O, beautiful one! My misery is similar to that of a starving man who, having delicious food placed before him, is forbidden to touch it. It is like the sufferings of a thirsty man who has sweet drinks within his reach but is not allowed to drink. If you command me, I shall happily spend my life at your feet as your slave."

Padmamali: You had abducted me at Mantri and uttered such flattering words earlier. You must have remembered my reply. Abusing your power, you have imprisoned my father, raided our village and captured me once again by force. I am compelled to tell you that you shall be disappointed if, after all this, you are expecting an answer other than what I gave you at Mantri.

Duryodhana: The arrow of Manmatha, the god of love, has pierced my heart and I have no time to reason the means through which I have obtained you. If you think it is unjust, I ask for your forgiveness. But, just give me a glance of mercy.

Padmamali: I am a helpless girl. Although I am your captive, I cannot bring myself to give the answer you expect fom me. The demon Ravana had abducted goddess Sita in this manner, but he also dared not touch her. In the end, he, along with his clan of demons, got eliminated. You have kept me confined here for the last few days: The memory of my parents and kinsfolk and the pangs of separation are still fresh. And, in the meanwhile, you have started troubling me.

Duryodhana: Those tales written in books are not to be taken seriously. I feel so miserable at not being able to get you that you must not blame me if I act like a man without a conscience.

Padmamali: If you stoop to the level -of a beast, your action will shake the seat of God in heaven. He will use His divine power to stop you. You have experienced it once before.

The sarcasm in the words of Padmamali made Duryodhana seethe in anger. His body trembled and his eyes, red from habitual intake of intoxicating stuff, seemed to send out sparks. The enormity of his wrath rendered him speechless. With difficulty, he managed to speak in a hoarse voice:

"Well, let us see where your God is at this moment?"

Saying so, he advanced towards Padmamali.

At this moment Jayanti sprang up from her seat and in one quick movement took out a sharp-edged dagger from her clothes. Raising the dagger, she said loudly:

"Devil! Beware! I am the daughter of the Gadanayak of Ghantashila. If you move one step further I shall plant this dagger in your chest."

Duryodhana had not seen Jayanti before. Her appearance startled and frightened him. It is mentioned earlier that Jayanti was not slim, but she had a well-proportioned figure. Her bright, wheatish complexion, round face and the boldness with which she brandished the dagger made Duryodhana imagine as if the Mother Earth had cleaved the ground and appeared in person to save the helpless girl.

"So, you are, the daughter of the Gadanayak. But why are you getting so angry?" He asked.

Jayanti: You have insulted and imprisoned my father. The sly fox that you are, you have stolen me from my home. I was in the lookout for an opportunity to avenge myself; which God has granted me today. I shall redden this dagger with your unholy blood and mete out to you the punishment you deserve.

But she did not have to act on her words. As Duryodhana moved about, scared, a noise was heard outside, and the next moment the house was filled with people. In the light of the torch, they could see Parikshita Singh coming towards them followed by Balabantaray.

When Parikshita Singh noticed Duryodhana, Padmamali and Jayanti, he could guess that Duryodhana was about to molest the girls. He thanked God that he had arrived at the right moment. Then he addressed Duryodhana in the following manner:

"Villain, I hoped that you had learnt a lesson from the punishment you received from me at Mantri and had given up your evil ways. But I find that you haven't changed at all. You need a prolonged punishment to atone for the sins you have committed."

He turned to his attendant: Balabantaray, send this man without delay to Kaptipada in the custody of guards.

Immediately, on receipt of the order, Balabantaray tied up Duryodhana strongly with a rope and landed two heavy blows on his back.

"Wicked man!" Balabantaray said. "Though I was innocent, you had beaten me without any reason. It had caused me immense pain. Today I have avenged that insult." He dragged Duryodhana away.

A palanquin was sent from the royal palace at the orders of Parikshita Singh. He set out to Berhampur along with Padmamali and Jayanti. Before leaving, he ordered the garden house of Duryodhana to be set on fire. Bali Babu raided the fort. He received an information that a platoon of British soldiers and a Subedar from Balasore were marching to Nilagiri and that they would arrive in the morning. Bali Babu, therefore, returned to Berhampur with his troop.

The Epilogue

By the time the British force arrived at Nilagiri, the rebels had escaped to Berhampur. The queen along with Ricketts Sahib reached there just after the arrival of the force. The Sahib restored peace and normalcy in Nilagiri. Then he chased the rebels. A troop of soldiers belonging to the rebel camp was guarding the road sitting around a fire on the way about a mile from Berhampur. The British forces arrived there and fired a few shots, one of which pierced the chest of Govinda Sardar Singh and killed him instantly. The rebels informed Hari Babu of the arrival of the British force and left the place in a hurry. The Sahib could not capture the rebels as they had already fled. But in their haste to leave, the rebels had left behind the empty palanquin of Padmamali and three horses. Realising that it would be useless to chase the rebels further, Rickets Sahib returned to Nilagiri and after establishing peace there, returned to Balasore ..

The sahib made an investigation of the incident of the raid of Panchagada and sentenced Santi Das to three years of rigorous imprisonment. Bhagirathi Pattnaik was fined two thousand and five hundred rupees and was to undergo two years imprisonment in case of default.

He also ordered for the removal of Panchagada from the rule of Nilagiri and placed it under the direct control of the government. The trial of the rebels began in time and Ricketts Sahib took a lot of pain to arrive at the truth. In the judgment he passed, Bali Babu and Hari Babu were sentenced to two years of imprisonment each. Parikshita Singh was sentenced to six months of imprisonment and the king of Mayurbhanja had to pay a fine of five hundred rupees.

The Sahib sought government approval for his judgment.

The Hon'ble Governor confirmed the above punishments. However, he issued orders for a reconsideration of the sentence relating to King Parikshita Singh only. Mahanta Harihara Ramanuja Das met Ricketts Sahib after such orders were received from the Governor's office. We do not know what exactly the Mahanta confidentially told Mr. Ricketts, but the Sahib was a little annoyed and said:

"Oh, so this was the case? Why didn't you tell me before? I am very displeased."

When Ricketts Sahib heard about Parikshita Singh and Padmamali, he dismissed his earlier order relating to Parikshita Singh and arranged for the marriage of the king with Padmamali.

The marriage was celebrated with great pomp and splendour. The king and Padmamali returned to Kaptipada. The subjects there rejoiced over the event for several days.

Since the time Padmamali was rescued at Nilagiri, Jayanti was engaged to wait on her. Balabantaray was also appointed as the head of the king's entourage. One day, while the king was passing a pleasant time in Padmamali's company, she told him:

"You are concerned only with your own happiness."

"Why do you say so?" the king asked. "What happened?"

"You have not taken any steps to bring happiness to those two who have helped us so much in difficult times," Padmamali remarked.

"What do you say?" Parikshita Singh said. "Which two people are you talking about?"

"Jayanti and Balabantaray."

"What about them? They do not have any problem here."

"Only a selfish person speaks like this," she said.

"I don't understand you. It is difficult to fathom a woman's thoughts. Who could say what miracles you could have performed had you not been born a woman?" the king said, jestfully.

"The true feelings of a woman are hardly ever understood by men," Padmamali retorted.

"Alright, I agree. Tell me what you want?"

"It is about Jayanti," Padmamali said.

"What about her?" the king asked.

"She is in love with Balabantaray."

King Parikshita could understand the matter now and organized their wedding in a grand manner. After the ceremony, both Jayanti and Balabantaray experienced intense joy and happiness in each other's company.

The readers might wonder what happened to Duryodhana. Since two charred bodies, one of a man and the other that of a woman were recovered from the debris of the garden house, people believed that Duryodharia was burnt to death at the garden house. But the man was one of the servants of Duryodhana and the woman was Ramia's mother. Duryoclhana remained for some time in the prison at Kaptipada, but he could not survive the excessive physical and mental strain for long and died.

Black Eagle Books

www.blackeaglebooks.org
info@blackeaglebooks.org

Black Eagle Books, an independent publisher, was founded as a nonprofit organization in April, 2019. It is our mission to connect and engage the Indian diaspora and the world at large with the best of works of world literature published on a collaborative platform, with special emphasis on foregrounding Contemporary Classics and New Writing.

www.ingramcontent.com/pod-product-compliance
Lightning Source LLC
Chambersburg PA
CBHW050404110726
47899CB00008B/2639